TISH

EDWINA WYATT
ILLUSTRATED BY ODETTE BARBEROUSSE

BERBAY
PUBLISHING

FOR HENRY AND AUDREY

PART 1

Somewhere

CHAPTER 1

In which Tish comes out of Nowhere

Have you ever heard of Tish? Tish, who was quick like a mongoose, but lazy like a bear? Tish, who was heavy like a mammoth, but had a heart like a feather? Tish, who had small, stumpy wings, and could *almost-nearly* fly? Tish, who cried so easily when he was happy or hungry or mad? Well, now you have. He is yours, too. Because Tish belongs to everybody, but especially to Charles Dimple. Which is only fair, since Charles was the one to dream him up in the first place.

Tish began as a spark. An idea. To start with, he was no more than a speck of gold dust. He floated on the wind. Bobbed across an ocean. Tumbled down a waterfall. Hurtling towards his destiny like a shooting star. When he finally arrived at 33 Sprinkle Street, damp and a little weary, it was late and Charles was in bed staring blankly at a page. His ginger curls falling over his eyes. His pencil hovering over an empty line.

There is something missing, he was thinking. But what is it?

The spark flickered on the windowsill, watching the small huddle of pajamas searching for an idea, unaware that one was right beside him. Creeping closer, the spark glimmered on Charles's shoulder, trying to see what he was making.

It was a list. Charles Dimple made a lot of lists (since, from his observations, ideas liked to stretch and sprawl across the page when they were just waking up).

This particular list was labeled: **THE PERFECT FRIEND**. Although it was more like a job description than a list. At the top of Charles's list were TUSKS. Tusks were important to Charles Dimple. Beneath TUSKS, was another word: BIG. His perfect friend would be BIG. And by BIG, Charles meant that his friend should be big enough to hide beneath in a storm. But not so big that he wouldn't fit on the top bunk (which is where he would sleep, if he promised to mind his tail and keep it clean; TAIL [being third on the list]). Furthermore, his perfect friend would have wisps of smoke that curled from his nostrils like the steam from a hot apple pie. A bit like a dragon—but better. Loyalty, honesty and politeness were also essential. Yet he shouldn't be too polite, just enough that he would snap the last chocolate-chip cookie in half and share it with you. But not so polite that he would say, "after you" when going through a door, or fail to tell you that you had parsley in your teeth. There should be feathers and fur. Perhaps some bristles like a hedgehog. A trunk for holding pencils or a berry-swirl waffle cone from Mr. Confetti's ice-cream truck. And an umbrella. Umbrellas were also important to Charles Dimple.

It's me, crackled the spark. *Or it could be.*

Glowing with excitement, the spark fizzed and hummed around Charles's head. *Pick me, pick me!*

Charles trapped it with his mind like a firefly in a jar. Once inside, something powerful began to take shape. The idea stretched and swelled until poof!

An image flashed before him. He saw someone. Or something. In his room. A sort of beast. It was a little wobbly and smudged around the edges. But here it was. His perfect friend. Well, almost perfect.

"Ack!" said Charles, seeing now what he was missing. "Wings!"

Charles stood on his bed and imagined a pair of wings for the beast. But there wasn't really much room in among all the other important bits. So he squashed a couple of small wings on the side and hoped for the best. His mouth fell open as he stepped back to admire his work. His glasses fogged up. He had never seen anything so grand. *So perfect.*

"Where did you come from?"

"Nowhere," mumbled the beast.

"Oh," said Charles. "Where's that?"

The beast wanted to explain that Nowhere was a place halfway between Curiosity and Courage. But he couldn't. For that, he would need a map; the heart is a vast place where one can easily get lost.

The beast shifted and swayed, sniffed Charles once, licked him on the ear, then plodded around the room, inspecting his new home. He poked into corners, nosed through an underwear drawer, knocked over chairs, and nibbled on an old sandwich he found in Charles's lunchbox.

He was a little smellier and rumblier than Charles had imagined, but overall, he couldn't want for more.

After introducing himself properly, and apologising for the state of his bedroom, Charles did up the top button on his pajamas. He wanted to look respectable, having reached the most significant part of the ceremony: the choosing of a name.

"So," asked Charles. "What name do you like? Terry? George? Top Deck? Fang?"

Charles was just about to suggest the name Montague when the beast thrust his snout into a vase of roses that Charles's mother had put beside his bed in the vain hope of masking the stench of his socks.

The beast's brow began to wrinkle. The whiskers on his chin quivered. Then he closed his eyes, opened his jaws and, "Ah-*tish!*"

He sneezed. At least he thought he did, but it only got halfway out before getting stuck. You know the ones—those awful explosions that are finished just as soon as they begin. Half a sneeze is always a disappointment, like coming home from a day at the beach with a dry bathing suit.

"Tish?" said Charles. "Tish. That is a good name."

And so it was that Tish got his name. It was not a grand name. He was not named after a stone castle or a lake or an opera singer.

"Tish," said the beast over and over, enjoying the crunchy feeling in his mouth. He let it linger on his tongue like a butterscotch ball.

"Tish, Tish, Tisssshhhhhh." He sloshed it around before swallowing it whole.

Charles passed him a handkerchief to dab his eyes and blow his trunk. Then he went downstairs to get them a snack.

Alone in Charles's room, Tish looked around. He inched towards the open window, staring into the black night. The curtains billowed around him. He pushed his head through and gazed out. A city spread before him, dotted with buildings like a picnic rug covered with ants. His tail quivered. The bristles on his neck stood up, sensing for danger. Then he heard a voice behind him.

"This is your new home," said Charles, returning with two glasses of milk, some slices of apple, and sprigs of parsley for decoration. "Thirty-three Sprinkle Street. And over the hill is your new school. Can you imagine?"

Tish could not imagine, having no imagination at all. He needed someone to do the imagining for him, which is the reason he had been waiting so long to get here.

Yet despite feeling sad about not being able to imagine his new school, he was very happy. So happy, in fact, that he rumbled until the floorboards shook and the pictures on the walls went crooked. He had dreamed of this moment for so long that it did not seem real. He nipped himself on the tail, just to check that he wasn't asleep. That he really was here.

Lifting his trunk, Tish breathed in the scents of Sprinkle Street: the vines of summer jasmine on the balcony, the hot noodles and spicy herbs from the cart below, the steamy, sudsy smells floating up from the laundromat next door. He leaned closer to Charles, trying to take everything in: the walls of ivy, the rows of terraced houses, the lines of traffic heading over the bridge. There were towers and apartments stacked up on top of each other like tins of tomato soup. There were parks with illuminated statues and sparkling fountains. They stood together for a long time, nibbling their apples and sipping their milk. Listening. Watching. Then Tish saw the moon. Like a round white plate in the sky. He stretched out his trunk and tried to touch it—to catch it. But he couldn't get a grip. He stepped back from the window and stared at Charles, his eyes bright and shining.

"Nice, isn't it?" said Charles. "I can teach you all the constellations." Constellations were important to Charles Dimple.

Tish gazed at the night sky. Then he glanced at Charles, moving closer to his face until they were eye to eye.

"What is it?" Charles took a step back.

"Parsley," said Tish. "In your teeth."

And from that moment, Charles made a promise to Tish that he would never let him go.

For he truly was the perfect friend.

CHAPTER 2

In which Tish
goes to school

Tish got down on both knees, suspiciously eyeing his breakfast. He was improving at using a straw, but he still couldn't understand what a fork was for.

"Spear it, like this." Charles rolled up a pancake and forked it into his mouth.

Tish curled his trunk around the handle and tried to do the same. The fork disappeared. He let out a muffled squeak.

Charles stood up from the table, ready to perform Emergency First Aid. He had read all about the Heimlich Maneuver in his encyclopedia but before he could get there Tish froze. His brow wrinkled. The whiskers on his chin quivered. He closed his eyes, opened his jaws and, "*Ah-tish-oo!*" The fork clattered to the ground in a gooey mess.

"*Grum, grum, grum,*" rumbled Tish, feeling much better, having found the other half of his sneeze. It had been stuck in his head all night.

Once Tish had returned to his normal color, Charles rushed about to get him ready for his first day of school. He scrubbed his face with a steamy washcloth. He combed the tufty mass of hairs on Tish's head.

"There," said Charles. "Now, where have all my socks gone?"

He dug through the washing basket on the kitchen table like an archeologist searching for dinosaur bones.

"Ack!" he said. "We're going to be late for school."

Tish cocked his ears.

"What does 'late' mean?" he asked through a mouthful of pancake.

"Late," said Charles, pointing to a cuckoo clock on the wall. "It means we won't get to school on time."

Tish stared at the clock, looking confused. He sniffed it all over. The bristles on his neck standing up. Then,

"*Cuckoo! Cuckoo! Cuckoo!*" A stuffed red bird flew out and blared in his face.

"Waaaah!" Tish dropped to his knees, hiding his eyes beneath his ears.

"Don't worry," said Charles, peeling back one of Tish's ears. "It can't hurt you. It's just a clock for telling the time."

But Tish did not understand time. "Can you eat time?" asked Tish.

Charles laughed and got out a piece of paper.

"We will miss the first school bus at this rate. But that's ok: cosmic theories are important."

He polished his glasses and drew a long arrow across the page.

"From my observations, time goes like this." Charles ran his finger across the page in the direction the arrow was pointing. "It does not go like this," he said, dragging his finger backwards along the arrow.

Tish followed Charles's finger with his eyes, his long lashes getting tangled up in each other with each slow blink.

"There's this theory," said Charles, "called the arrow of time. How the past is different from the future. How we remember the past, but we don't remember the future."

Tish licked the arrow. It didn't taste very nice. Charles got up and looked in the fridge.

"Are you still hungry?"

Tish nodded. He always got hungry when he was confused.

Charles poked around until he found a carton of eggs.

"Look at it this way," he said, cracking one into a bowl. "There are things that happen. *Irreversible processes...*" He turned on the frypan and melted a small pat of butter. "Like how you can turn an egg into an omelette." He whisked the egg and added a splash of milk. "But you can't turn an omelette back into an egg."

Charles poured the mixture into the hot pan. The smell of butter and eggs made Tish's mouth water. He watched as Charles flipped the egg into the air and caught it in the frypan. It didn't look like an egg anymore. Tish waited patiently as Charles cut it into thin slices and covered it with tomato sauce.

"Try," said Charles, cleaning the steam from his glasses. Tish leaned in and nibbled a piece. "No, Tish," chuckled Charles, "I mean try and turn the omelette back into an egg."

Tish stared at the omelette. "Womelette," he said, narrowing his eyes and unable to speak properly on account of all the dribble, "be a peg!"

But the omelette just sat there looking delicious. Next, he tried rolling the omelette into the shape of an egg. Although that didn't work either. So he got a fresh egg out of the carton and held it above the plate in his mouth to show the omelette what to do. But the egg had changed. Tish frowned at the omelette. Then *crack*! He'd squeezed the egg too tight in his jaws. A sticky stream of orange yolk pooled from Tish's mouth onto the kitchen floor like a puddle of sunshine. Tish bellowed and burst into tears. He dropped to his knees and tried scooping up the yolk to put it back in the shell.

"It's ok," said Charles, patting Tish on the neck. "Here, eat this."

Tish dried his eyes, licked Charles on the ear, then wolfed down the omelette in one great gulp. The dish was warm, but he felt an icy chill settle somewhere deep inside him. Because in that moment, Tish felt that Charles was wrong. That time *could* hurt you. Although he wasn't sure how. He did not like that bird, with its unseeing eyes and flightless wings; birds should sing and soar. Birds were beautiful. He did not like that broken egg.

"Aha!" called Charles, fishing out a pair of mismatched socks from beneath the couch.

"Let's put these on and go!"

Carrying Charles's backpack, Tish followed Charles down Sprinkle Street to the bus stop on the corner. The backpack was too small to fit on Tish's back, so he hung it from a tusk. Tusks are useful like that. Cars whooshed by, spattering them with drops of dirty water. Tish took a slurp from a puddle. Nibbled on some shrubs and bushes. Got his nose stuck in a letterbox and made friends with a snail. When the bus arrived, the seats were too small for Tish. So, he rode up top on the roof, his tail hanging down beside Charles's window, all ruffled up like a chimney brush.

The bell was ringing as the bus pulled up outside the school. Tish had never seen so many children before. His heart was pounding; his eyes grew misty. Staying close to Charles, Tish followed the stream of children flowing into the building as though riding a current downstream. Every now and then he saw the flick of a tail or the curve of a spike, as some of the other students in the third grade rushed inside with their very own friend of the Perfect kind to carry their backpacks. Some carried them between their teeth. Some dragged them along the ground. Others flew with them above their heads. And just like every backpack looked different, so too did the Perfects. Some had ten feet and some had ten eyes. There were frills and gills. Tutus and tiaras. But they all had one thing in common: they had each found their Someone. And in their Someone's eyes, they were perfect. Tish tried to count how many other Perfects there were. Although he had to stop when he reached twenty, not having enough toes to continue.

On Charles's signal, Tish trotted into a bright classroom and sat on the floor beside Charles's desk. As they waited for class to begin, Charles opened up his notebook to a fresh page and ruled a neat margin. Tish leaned over his shoulder, trying to see what he was making. It was a list. A new list called: **THINGS TO DO TOGETHER**, as most things are made better by being shared.

The list began with all the things that they had already done together, so that they could check them off one by one. Since, from Charles's observations, checking things *off* a list was even better than putting them *on*.

So far, the list looked like this:

> **THINGS TO DO TOGETHER**
> Make a list
> Make a pancake stack
> Invent a cosmic theory
> Ride the bus

Although Charles hadn't quite invented what he would be calling "Egg Theory," he felt it was only fair that he should claim it, having been the first to try it out with tomato sauce.

Tomato sauce was important to Charles Dimple. As Charles began checking off items with his red pen, there was a snigger from behind. A group of students were staring and pointing at Charles's list. The bristles on Tish's neck stood to attention like soldiers ready for battle. Then a hand reached across and scratched him behind the ears. Tish glanced back, his anger being replaced by something more tender. Not one of those kids had a Perfect curled up at their feet, hiding in their pocket or breathing fire in the corner. He licked Charles's hand and turned in a few circles before settling down for a nap, his hot apple-pie puffs curling around Charles's ankles. Rumbling quietly to himself, he drifted off to sleep on a cloud of sweet, happy thoughts.

CHAPTER 3

In which Tish goes to the park

By Saturday morning, Tish and Charles had already ticked five items off their list of **THINGS TO DO TOGETHER**.

"Look for fossils," said Charles, his red pen poised. "*Check.* Build a fort, dig a tunnel, make a metal detector, find a secret trapdoor—*check, check, check, check!*"

The next thing on the list was to visit the park. In particular, the swings.

Swings were important to Charles Dimple. When they got there, the park was empty and Charles gave Tish his first lesson in swinging.

"Like this?" asked Tish, kicking out his legs.

"Forward and back! Forward and back!" called Charles from the sky.

Tish tried to bend his knees like Charles was showing him. But his legs were too short. His bottom was too big. And his tail was too stuck. The swing buckled and groaned with the weight of him, as Charles whooshed back and forth besides him like a pendulum.

"Imagine you are flying! Up, up, up!"

Tish closed his eyes and tried to imagine. It wasn't much use. Firstly, because he didn't *have* an imagination. And secondly, because only that morning they had discovered that Tish *could* fly, but only like a chicken; lurching a few feet off the ground, flapping vigorously before landing in a rosebush. *Flap. Flap. Whee. Flap. Flap. Whoa. Flap. Flap. Whump.* Charles had almost struck: GO FLYING off the list, when it occurred to him, the swings at the park were the next best thing.

"Up!" pleaded Tish. "Up!" The swing only dragged along the ground, sending Charles into the air as though they were on a seesaw.

"You'll get the hang of it," said Charles.

Tish wasn't so sure. He didn't much like swinging, no matter how good Charles said it was.

After Charles grew tired of swinging, they walked through the park to try and tick something else off the list, namely: **eat a berry-swirl waffle cone.** According to Charles, this was the most urgent item on the list, and the only one written in bold letters with an underline. Finding a berry-swirl waffle cone was not a simple matter. The problem being that Mr. Confetti's ice-cream truck only arrived when it felt like it. And always at the oddest times and in the oddest places. Like during a blizzard, when your nose was too cold and your hands were too frozen to hold a berry-swirl waffle cone. Or in a quiet back alley that you only ever ventured down if you lost your cat or your tennis ball.

Yet Charles would always buy one, no matter when or where Mr. Confetti popped up. Since who knew when you might get the chance again—when you would get to taste that sweet burst of raspberries and vanilla?

There was nothing quite so good in all the world. But you didn't choose the flavor you wanted—Mr. Confetti chose it for you. He had a knack for knowing just what it was that you needed. The perfect flavor for you. And if you guessed right when he flipped your coin, you never had to pay.

"Heads or tails?" Mr. Confetti would say as he polished your coin on his candy-striped coat. Charles always chose tails, naturally. Tails being important to Charles Dimple, as we know.

"From my observations," said Charles, "Mr. Confetti does not drive the ice-cream truck. It's the *truck* that drives Mr. Confetti. So, if we are to find the truck, we first need to *think* like a truck."

Tish slumped on the grass. His legs were tired and his bottom was sore.

"If you were an ice-cream truck, where would you go?" asked Charles.

Tish closed his eyes and tried to think like an ice-cream truck. But having never *been* an ice-cream truck (so far as he knew) it was impossible. Besides, he didn't really know many places around here at all. He could count them on his toes: Sprinkle Street, the kitchen, the school, Charles's bedroom, and now the park.

After traveling around the perimeter, first forwards, then backwards, Tish and Charles sat under a tree and tried to come up with a new strategy. The sun was warm, the grass was soft, and there were so many beautiful birds twittering in the trees that Tish felt himself drifting off into a happy dream again.

"Tish?" Charles leaned over and peeled back one of his ears to check he was listening. Then he jerked back, wrinkling his nose. "*Ack!* What have you been rolling in?"

Tish rumbled sheepishly to himself. The answer being *everything*. Leaves. Garbage. Mud. His new body was useful, but it was also itchy and took some getting used to.

"You need a bath."

Tish trotted behind Charles as they searched for a large puddle or a duck pond that would be deep enough for Tish to have a wash. He kept his eyes peeled for any sign of Mr. Confetti as they went. In the middle of the park they found a fountain.

"Perfect!" said Charles, taking off his backpack and rolling up his sleeves.

"Where?" said Tish, looking around for one of his own kind—another Perfect.

"No, silly, I mean the fountain will make the perfect bath."

Tish sniffed the water and dipped in a toe.

The fountain was filled with stone cherubs with dimply arms and legs. Tish liked those cherubs. They had stumpy little wings just like his.

"Are you coming in too?" he asked.

Charles did not answer. He was watching a group of children sitting on the other side. Tish recognized them from class. He thumped his tail. They looked so happy sitting there, the tops of their heads catching the sun. Their reflections danced together in the water with Charles's, although above the surface, their eyes had not even reached him. Not one of them looked at Charles. Not one of them said hello. Tish couldn't understand why. It was as though Charles wasn't there at all. As though Charles Dimple were invisible.

Charles stood up and put his backpack back on.

"Come on," he said, a shadow falling over his face.

"No bath?" asked Tish, trying to pin down a rainbow in the water with his foot.

"Maybe later."

"Want a hairy-twirl snuffle cone?" said Tish, his trunk full of water.

"Not now," said Charles.

Tish followed Charles home through the park. At the crossing, Charles paused to wait for the walk signal. His shoulders were slouched, his head drooped. Tish shuffled closer, thumping his tail on the cement. He nibbled Charles's hair. He licked him on the ear. And just like that the shadow lifted from Charles's face. When the signal changed from red to green, Charles took off.

"Too slow!" he called, as he set in to race.

Tish wailed and loped along Sprinkle Street trying to catch him. *Flap. Flap. Whee. Flap. Flap. Whoa. Flap. Flap. Whump.*

CHAPTER 4

In which Tish has a bath

"Tish!" panted Charles as he climbed the stairs to 33 Sprinkle Street. "You're so quick! Like a mongoose! I couldn't believe it when you overtook me like that!"

"Why couldn't you believe it?"

"It's just you're usually so...sleepy. And a little... lazy. More like a bear."

Tish puffed up his chest with pride. He was *very* sleepy. And *especially* lazy.

"What's a mongoose?"

"It's a longish, furry creature with a pointy nose and a bushy tail. People *think* they are rodents but they are not."

"What are they?"

"They are members of the Herpestidae family like civets and meerkats. *And...* " Charles took a breath, "they are legendary snake fighters!"

"Oh," said Tish, impressed. "How do you know?"

"I read all about them in the museum. They are endangered, you know, like the polar bears. Also, Rikki-Tikki-Tavi is a mongoose. Do you know that story?" Tish didn't. "Come on, I'll read it to you in the bath."

"What's endangered mean?" asked Tish, trying not to be nervous about the bath, since it seemed that "later" was coming sooner than he had expected.

"It's when a species is threatened, but not extinct," said Charles, leading Tish into the bathroom and turning on the taps in the tub. "Some say it's only a matter of time before there are no more mongooses in the world."

"What do you say?" asked Tish.

"I say, there is still hope."

Tish peered into the bath, his bottom lip quivering at the sight of the tub filling up with water. Steam filled the room, and the pipes creaked and groaned as they always did when the hot water was on. Tish had never had a bath before. There was something strange floating across the top. He yelped and hid under the bath mat as best he could.

"Don't worry," said Charles. "It's just a rubber duck." In his arms he held a towel, a pink frilly shower cap, a scrubbing brush and a book. Tish peeked over the edge of the tub and nudged the yellow duck with his trunk. There seemed to be a lot of pretend birds in this house, popping up when he least expected them. He chewed on his shower cap for consolation.

"That's not for *eating*," said Charles, pulling the cap out of Tish's mouth.

"What's it for then?" asked Tish, eyeing the bath suspiciously. The duck was bobbing towards him.

"It's for keeping your hair dry."

Tish looked down. His whole body was covered with hair, so he wasn't quite sure why some bits should be kept dry while others were allowed to get wet. Yet he stooped to let Charles put it on, seeing as he appeared to be an expert in such matters. His hair *was* very nice, so red and curly.

Squeezing into the tub, Tish munched on the soap, while Charles made him a bubble beard. Then

Charles made one for himself, spreading foamy whiskers all down his neck until he looked more like Father Christmas than an eight-year-old boy.

"*Grum, grum, grummm,*" Tish rumbled as Charles washed behind his ears, and scratched the itchy bits with the scrubbing brush. When his tusks were polished, his toenails brushed and his knots unpicked, Tish leaned back and soaked in the tub while Charles experimented with a new hairstyle in the mirror. Then Charles dragged in a chair and began reading *Rikki-Tikki-Tavi*. Tish was just about to say that he had never felt so relaxed in all his life when *crack!* The tub split in two.

"Ack!" said Charles, jumping back as water began seeping out the sides. The rubber duck shot past, navigating the white-water rapids that coursed through the bathroom.

"Charles!" called a voice from downstairs. "Is everything all right?"

"Fine!" called Charles, making a dam out of towels and channeling the water down the drain. "Just fine!"

"Sorry," moaned Tish, tears spilling down his cheeks.

"Don't be," said Charles, rubbing the towel behind his ears. "Everyone here takes showers. Who needs a bath anyway?"

Tish nodded and bit his bottom lip, trying to stop it from trembling. Charles really was the perfect friend. Patient, understanding, and kind. Knowing just when to stretch the truth that little bit further, and when to snap it right back into shape. Together they looked for a towel big enough to dry the rest of him, but they were all too small.

"Wait a moment," said Charles. "I'll get my blanket."

But it was too late. Tish shook. And shook. And *shook*. Until every corner of the bathroom was sodden again. After they had cleaned up and dressed in their pajamas, Tish and Charles went downstairs for dinner.

Tish had never met Charles's mother before. He smiled his biggest smile and tried not to smell the roses on the table in case he sneezed again. His long tongue began to quiver as Charles scooped out some mashed potatoes for him. He sniffed the fluffy white boulders then swallowed them in one gulp, plate and all.

"Plates are not for eating," whispered Charles, whisking away the salad bowl before he could eat that too. Luckily for Tish, Charles's mother didn't seem to notice there was one less plate at the table.

"Did you make any new friends this week, Charlie?"

Charles built a castle of peas. He made a moat with tomato sauce and floated a sausage boat along the top. He built a drawbridge and a dungeon. "One," he said, and gave Tish a shy smile.

"One is all you need."

After dinner, Tish could smell something delicious. But it was not in the bowl of banana yogurt in front of him, although that was very nice. It was something Charles's mother was eating. Something small and green and crunchy that she cracked out of a shell. Tish's nose sniffed and snuffed so much that it puffed out apple-pie wisps of smoke the size of storm clouds.

"What are those?" Tish whispered to Charles under the table.

Charles wrinkled his nose. "Pistachios."

"Pistachios," Tish repeated. Even the word tasted good. He reached towards the bowl in the middle of the table with his trunk. The hairs on his chin trembled the closer that he got.

"I wouldn't," said Charles, sticking out his tongue and crossing his eyes. "They are *yuck!*"

Tish peeled his trunk back along the table. "Not delicious?"

"From my observations, pistachios are the very worst, most disgusting sort of food."

"Oh," said Tish.

"*Horrible.*" Charles shivered. "Awful."

"Oh yes, *scorrible*," repeated Tish, trying not to dribble too much. "Clawful."

Although something told Tish that pistachios were not horrible or awful at all.

"So, what do you think of your new home?" Charles's mother asked. "And your new school?"

"Blunderful!" said Tish, fishing out a piece of willow-patterned china from his front teeth. Then Tish realized: Charles's mother wasn't asking him. She was asking *Charles.*

Charles poked at his food for a while. When he spoke it didn't sound like him. It was like he was only halfway there—his voice was small and faraway.

"Not bad," he said.

"But not *good*?"

Charles shrugged and his mom sighed.

"You must be missing your dad and your old friends, but they will visit. And one day, you will wake up and things will feel normal and familiar again. It's only a matter of time."

Charles nodded and sat in silence. And Tish realized another thing: that Charles was trying to find Somewhere too. Trying to build a new life for himself, just like Tish. And when Tish looked at Charles, he sensed that Charles *knew* things would get better, in that large and logical part of his brain. But that sometimes, just like Tish, he also had trouble imagining.

CHAPTER 5

In which Tish
asks a question

By the time autumn came, Tish had grown a whole loaf wider, his coat had grown a whole hand deeper, and his snores had grown a whole trunk louder. His wings, however, had stayed the same. (Although he had gotten much better at flying and could travel almost the entire length of Sprinkle Street, even if he was only a meter off the ground.)

According to Charles, Tish could no longer sleep inside but had to sleep outside in the garden. This had surprised Tish, since for months, Charles had not been able to sleep without Tish rumbling above him on the top bunk. But they still shared a glass of milk and some apple slices decorated with parsley every night before bed.

At first, Tish had been afraid outside on his own. After a few nights, he realized he was not alone. The sounds and smells of the city kept him company, the vines and the ivy, the sizzling noodles, the hum of the laundromat next door. When he couldn't sleep, he counted the windows in the rows of terraced houses and the cars heading over the bridge, always keeping an eye out for Mr. Confetti and his ice-cream truck. And then there were the dogs and cats of Sprinkle Street that wandered around each night, although much like everybody else, they didn't seem to notice Tish.

"Do you hear someone?" he once heard a cat hiss in a back alley.

"There's no one there," another called back.

Things started to change in other places too, like school. One lunchtime, as Tish looked around the playground, he couldn't see as many Perfects as usual. He counted all the students to make sure they were all there. And they were. But their Perfects were not. It didn't much matter to Tish;

the other Perfects had kept their distance, but for the odd nod or occasional wave.

When he had first arrived at school, Tish had wondered why they couldn't all be friends. After all, they would have a lot to talk about. He finally figured out it was an unsaid rule that you didn't go too near another Perfect's Someone in case you let off a spark and gave their person a better idea. Although Tish never worried about that. He was sure Charles would never replace him and think that someone else's Perfect was more perfect than him. Charles had dreamed him up, after all. Besides, none of the others had tusks.

"Where did the others go?" Tish finally asked a small, pink Perfect scuttling past.

She was long and low to the ground with spotty paws, as though a sausage dog had got mixed up with a batch of cotton candy.

"Somewhere Else," she said quickly, moving away.

"Where is that?" Tish called after her.

"I can't imagine," she said, lowering her voice, her eyes darting around.

Neither could Tish.

"But it's only a matter of time," she added.

Time, thought Tish. There is that word again.

"What is?"

"It's only a matter of time before we are there too."

The lunch bell rang and Tish watched her dash off. The bristles on the back of his neck were standing up. He shook off the icy chill closing in on him and hurried to catch up with Charles. Back in the classroom, Tish curled up beside Charles's desk and tried to go to sleep. But his thoughts were keeping him awake. He looked across the room to the small, pink creature sitting in her Someone's lap. Whatever did she mean? Where were they going?

Tish closed his eyes and let his worries wisp away in a puff of smoke, since he decided he wasn't going anywhere. Not unless it was with Charles.

CHAPTER 6

In which Tish
makes a mistake

One morning, when Tish and Charles were having breakfast, they had their first misunderstanding. Although it was only afterwards that Tish realized that this was what had happened. It began when Charles took out his red pen and started checking items off their list of **THINGS TO DO TOGETHER**.

"Visit the library," said Charles. "*Check.*"

Tish nibbled his toast and bowed his head. They *had* visited the library, although they hadn't stayed long, since Tish had got confused about the difference between *borrowing* a book and *eating* one.

"Go to the pool," continued Charles with a flourish of his pen. "*Check.*"

Tish flushed red, his tail wedged between his legs. They *had* gone to the local swimming pool, yet it had closed soon after, since Tish had got confused about the difference between sitting in the pool and sitting on the toilet.

"Jump on the trampoline," said Charles. "*Check.*"

As Charles continued reading, Tish attempted to curl himself into a small ball. After some effort, it wasn't so much a ball as an enormous boulder. He pulled his favorite tea cozy off the bench, the one with the pom pom, and wore it as a hat to help him hide. Because, of course, they *had* jumped on the trampoline. He shuddered, the image playing over and over in his mind: *Flap. Flap. Whee. Flap. Flap. Whoa. Flap. Flap. Crack!*

Charles had not been angry. In the same way he hadn't been angry about the broken egg, the broken swing, or the broken bath.

"Who needs trampolines anyway?" he had said. But Tish could tell that while Charles wasn't angry, he was something else. Something *worse*. Something that made Tish's head droop and shoulders sag.

It had taken a while for Tish to figure it out, but then he understood. Charles was disappointed. Since while Tish was the perfect friend, there was something important that Charles had forgotten to imagine in the beginning when he had chosen Tish. He had forgotten to imagine the future. What it would be like to do all his favorite things with a giant, woolly, rumbly beast with almost-nearly wings. And not someone more like him, Charles. Because even though Tish could breathe apple-pie smoke a-bit-like-a-dragon-but-*better* out of his nostrils, there were some things he and Charles would never be able to do together.

"So, Tish," said Charles, checking his watch, "we still have to go to the aquarium, the ice rink and toast some marshmallows. But today..." Charles paused for dramatic effect, "today, let's go to the museum."

Tish opened his eyes. He sat up and let his tail come out. Charles had told him all about the museum. Museums were important to Charles.

"Tish?" said Charles. "What do you think?"

But Tish did not answer. Sensing there was a problem, Charles got out the list again.

"Or if you don't feel like doing that, we could play cricket, find a spider's nest, or look for tadpoles?"

Tish stayed under his tea cozy. And it was lucky that he did, as, "*Cuckoo! Cuckoo! Cuckoo!*" The stuffed red bird flew out and blared through the house. Tish's tail shot straight back between his legs and he pulled the tea cozy even further over his eyes.

"Nine o'clock!" said Charles, looking at the clock. "The museum doors will be opening soon. If we're going, we should go now before it gets too busy."

Tish felt his feather-light heart growing heavy. He wanted to go with Charles, but he didn't want to spoil the day. Again.

Charles came closer and looked over the top of his glasses at Tish. He put the back of his hand to Tish's forehead and took his temperature. And when he was satisfied that Tish was not sick, he put two sandwiches into his backpack and an orange for later.

"Come on, get up."

But Tish didn't get up.

"Tish? Don't you want to come?"

Tish stayed silent. Charles pulled on his shoes and did up his laces.

"Shake once for yes. And twice for no."

Tish shook his pom pom twice.

"Really?" said Charles. "Ok."

But Tish could tell that he had disappointed Charles. Again. He watched as Charles put on his backpack and walked away.

"See you later," said Charles, and closed the door.

"Goodbye," said Tish.

CHAPTER 7

In which Tish
visits the museum

As soon as Charles had left, Tish realized that he had made a mistake. He shook off his tea cozy and bundled out the door. For a creature as heavy as Tish, he was surprisingly quick on his feet. Gathering speed on the downward slope, he took a running jump at the bottom of Sprinkle Street and launched himself off the ground. He scudded once, twice, three times across the path, then he was up! To anybody watching, they would have thought a large gust of wind was surging through the street. Since being only a few feet off the ground, his tail dragged beneath him, whipping up rubbish, stirring up leaves and knocking off hats.

When Tish arrived at the museum (*Flap. Flap. Whee. Flap. Flap. Whoa. Flap. Flap. Ouch.*), he was greeted by a large polar bear. The bristles on his neck stood up as he stared into its noble eyes. Then a woman pushed in front of him, blocking his view.

"And here is another endangered species," she said to a large group that stood around her in a circle, "on the brink of becoming extinct."

"What does that mean?" asked a girl. Her eyes were wide and frightened.

"Soon they will all be gone. Some say it's only a matter of time."

Tish went to say something, since she had forgotten to add the most important part—the part about hope. But he stumbled back and bumped into a wall. Fortunately, there was only a map on this particular wall, and not precious sculpture or tapestry.

Tish gulped as he tried to work out where he was. The museum was enormous. Charles could be anywhere. Deciding to start with Charles's favorite interest, he took off in the direction of the space exhibition.

Then he stopped. What if Charles hadn't got to it yet, and Tish missed him? Tish decided to start at the beginning, and went straight through a door labeled "WILD." Crowds of people filled every corner of the room, staring into glass cabinets that lined each wall. Tish went past a lion, a panda and an eagle. He found an ostrich, a rhinoceros, a peacock, and a giant tortoise. He looked for a mongoose, although he couldn't find one.

"Good morning," he said to each animal.

But they didn't answer back, only stared at Tish with their unseeing eyes like the little red bird that lived inside the clock.

Tish passed through a hall of dinosaurs and a room full of butterflies. Got stuck for a moment in a giant web with a big, hairy spider. Traveled back through 3,000 years of Egyptian history, past ancient relics, tapestries and carvings. Skidded through a garden. Got lost in a maze. Stumbled through a room full of armor and helmets and cowered in the middle of a parade of armed soldiers on horseback bearing flags and weapons. Found a room full of masks. A room full of money. A room full of blades and plaques, jade carvings and pots.

He passed gilded sculptures, mosaics and walls of stained glass. He walked beneath a roof made of glass. He went inside a tomb full of mummies. And deep into an ant colony. He became part of a living food chain and watched a documentary on decomposition. He went through a labyrinth and took a journey through someone's mind, traveling through emotions, memories, thoughts and dreams. He stood beside a famous horse and watched a crackly, black-and-white film of it winning a race. At the end of it all, at least he hadn't broken or destroyed anything. Right at that moment, when Tish didn't know whether to laugh or cry, he found Charles.

He was sitting on a bench outside, kicking leaves with his feet, staring up at the clouds.

"Tish!" he called, running towards him. "You came!"

Tish flew towards Charles. *Flap. Flap. Oh! Flap. Flap. Ho! Flap. Flap. Ha!*

Dropping to his knees, Tish bowed as Charles threw his arms around him, burying his face in the soft patch of fur on his chest. Tish rumbled so loudly that the earth shook beneath their feet. Once they had both apologized for whatever it was that had happened, Charles got up and led Tish over to the bench. His glasses all fogged up with excitement.

"Did you see the dinosaurs and the prehistoric horses? Did you read that a female house fly can lay up to 600 eggs at a time and each egg can become an adult in about two weeks? And did you know that one in every three mouthfuls of food we eat and beverages we drink are delivered to us by pollinators?"

Tish licked Charles on the ear. He hadn't seen him so happy since the day he had first arrived. Then his nose twitched. He licked him again. Then again. On the cheek this time. Charles tasted *delicious*. Like fresh summer berries and...vanilla?

"Oh, Tish, you just missed him!"

"Missed who?"

"Mr. Confetti! The ice-cream truck was right here. I couldn't believe it! I wanted to get you a berry-swirl waffle cone, but it would have melted by the time I got home. Sorry."

Just then, Tish heard a *crack* and thought that it was perhaps his heart, breaking in two. But it was only the bench they were sitting on. He landed with a thud on the cold, hard cement.

"Next time," said Tish.

"Next time," said Charles.

CHAPTER 8

In which Tish
makes a discovery

As autumn turned to winter, Tish was unable to ride on top of the bus to school. It was too wet and snowy.

Charles came up with a solution: Tish could walk on his own, under his umbrella, and meet him there.

"On my own?" asked Tish, his tail drooping. "Without you?"

"You will be fine!"

But Tish wasn't worried about himself. He was happy to walk alone. He loved seeing his big track marks in the snow and finding crunchy, frozen leaves. He was worried because up until now, Charles hadn't liked riding the bus alone. Sensing Tish was worried, Charles came up with another solution.

"Or you can stay at home, if you like. Take the day off."

"No thank you," said Tish, his tail sinking a little lower. He did not want to take the day off. Not unless it was with Charles. "I will walk."

Tish put on his tea cozy and went out into the snow. The wind blew his umbrella inside out. Then it blew his whiskers inside out. An icy chill settled upon his ears and wrapped around his neck, but Tish plodded on until he saw the school. As he waited for Charles's bus to arrive, Tish looked out for the other Perfects; for the flick of a tail or the curve of a spike. But he couldn't see one. Not even the little pink sausage dog.

They must be coming on the bus, thought Tish. He swayed from side to side, trying to keep warm. He hummed a little tune. Then he heard the squeak of brakes as the bus arrived.

Tish saw Charles in the window and sighed with relief. He watched through the window as Charles put on his backpack and walked down the steps. He called out to Charles. But Charles didn't call back. He was too busy talking to someone else. Someone who *wasn't* Charles, but who was so *like* Charles, that Tish had to blink to make sure he wasn't seeing double. They laughed at the same time. Stepped at the same time. Stopped at the same time. Shook their heads at the same time. They did everything together, just as he and Charles did.

Tish grinned. It made him happy to see Charles with a new friend. They could all go to the park together. To the museum. Maybe even get a berry-swirl waffle cone each if they were lucky. And then Tish noticed something else. The boy that Charles was walking with didn't have a Perfect. In fact, not one of the children walking into class had a Perfect with them. And not one Perfect had stepped off the bus.

Tish turned in a circle, his eyes darting around. They must all be inside. But he could tell by the number of students tearing around the playground, making snowmen and hurling ice at each other that they weren't. And then something hit Tish hard like a snowball in the chest.

Charles said goodbye to his new friend and ran over to Tish.

"Are you ok, boy?" he said, ruffling the downy fluff behind Tish's ears. "You look a little pale."

Tish nodded. But he wasn't ok. A familiar icy chill was flooding through him. Although this time, it wasn't in his ears or around his neck, but right down in his heart. Because there was no denying it. No burying the sad truth beneath a lie or a tea cozy. They were all gone. Just like the polar bear in the museum, Tish and all his kind were endangered—on the brink of becoming extinct. Tish felt the bristles on his neck stand up. He began to fret and pace. Turning in circles and marching on the spot.

Had the others done something wrong? Was there anything he could do to bring them back?

Then he froze as a new wave of realization crashed over the top of him. If they are all gone, he thought, I am the last one.

"Tish?" asked Charles.

Tish looked at Charles, looked deep into his heart. And that was when he knew. He knew that one day he would be gone from this place too. And Charles would not be coming with him.

CHAPTER 9

In which Tish wins a race and loses a friend

Despite Tish's discovery, life went on. Charles and Tish made snowmen and scarecrows. Played ping-pong and chess. They went to the aquarium and the ice rink, they camped in the forest and toasted marshmallows. And they read the last page of *Rikki-Tikki-Tavi*. There was only one thing left to do on the list. Tish wondered if they would ever get to tick off that last item together.

It was the day of Charles's birthday and he received a ticket for the cinema. Tish was excited. He had never been to the movies before.

When they arrived, Charles and Tish fidgeted on the red carpet in the line outside the building. The air was filled with the salty, buttery scent of fresh popcorn—and something else even more fragrant: something nutty and familiar. Tish looked behind him and saw someone eating something out of a packet.

Something small and green and crunchy that she cracked out of a shell.

Tish recognized them right away: pistachios! Charles saw them too. "*Yuck*," he whispered, wrinkling his nose.

"Yes," said Tish, his stomach rumbling like thunder. "*Horrible*."

Tish thumped his tail on the red carpet as a woman lifted up the golden rope outside the entrance to let them in. As they went inside, the crowds of people disappeared through small doors and dark tunnels, until it was only Tish and Charles. When they reached the door that had the same number on it as the ticket, they followed a line of steep stairs lit by tiny lights like stars, that seemed to stretch into space. With nobody else inside, Charles was free to pick the seat that he liked the best. He chose one right at the front in the middle. It was cozy in there, nestled between the blue velvet drapes and gold frames. Tish looked up and saw a dangling crystal chandelier floating above them. Charles lowered himself into a thick, plush seat and Tish spread out on the carpet. The lights went down.

"It's about to start!" whispered Charles, although he didn't know why he was whispering, since there was no one to hear but them.

Tish nodded and took a deep breath. There was a sort of magic that crackled in the air as they sat together in the dark, waiting to go on an adventure. The curtains drew back and right in the middle of the stage was a van. It sat there, still and silent.

Tish looked at Charles. He didn't know it was a movie about vans. It seemed like a strange sort of movie, and nowhere near as exciting as he had thought it would be.

A tray flipped down, a window zoomed open and a face poked out. Inside the window were rows and rows of ice-cream, glistening like jewels, in every flavor imaginable.

"What'll it be?" said a man, jumping out.

Charles knew exactly who the man was.

"Two berry-swirl waffle cones, please, Mr. Confetti!" he said, his eyes like two giant scoops of hazelnut gelato.

On the way home from the cinema, Charles seemed quiet. Tish thought he must have been tired, having laughed so hard during the movie that tears had streamed down his cheeks.

He had stopped laughing quite so loud when a group of kids arrived later. They had missed the beginning, and Mr. Confetti had gone by then, but they seemed to have enjoyed sitting up the back, munching on popcorn and slurping on their drinks. When the lights came up, Charles's face didn't look the same as it had when they first arrived. His eyes weren't as bright and his shoes seemed too heavy. And despite the fact that they were going home to have Charles's favorite birthday lunch, he didn't seem excited about it.

At the crossing, Tish shuffled closer, thumping his tail on the cement. He nibbled Charles's hair. He licked him on the ear. But the shadow didn't lift from Charles's face as it usually did. It was as though his magic had run out. When the signal changed from red to green, Tish took off as they always did to race.

"Too slow!" he called, loping up the street ahead of him. When he arrived at 33 Sprinkle Street, Charles wasn't there. Tish waited on the step. And after what seemed like a lifetime, he saw Charles plodding up the street. Stranger still, he was calling for Tish, even though Tish was right there.

"Charles!" called Tish, bouncing up and down. "Over here!"

But Charles went on calling.

"Charles! Here, over here!"

When Charles finally walked up the stairs to the front door, Tish licked him on the ear and rubbed his head on his chest.

"Tish?" asked Charles, a blank look coming over his face.

"I'm here," said Tish.

Charles looked at Tish, stared deep into his eyes. And Tish looked at Charles, staring deep into his heart. Tish didn't like what he found. It sent him staggering back, made him drop to his knees. Charles Dimple could not see him. No matter how hard he looked. Even though Tish was standing right there before him. The very last imaginary friend.

They kept standing there together, searching for each other, when the silence was broken.

"Charles?" asked a voice.

"Oh, hey."

Charles turned around and waved at a boy. It was the boy from the bus. Tish watched as Charles searched the empty stair in front of him once more before walking away. The boy took Charles across the road and introduced him to a group of kids. Tish recognized them. They were the kids he saw sitting on the fountain the first time Charles had taken him to the park. Like magic, Tish watched the shadow lift from Charles's face as the kids gathered around and sang him "Happy Birthday." Because Charles had found Somewhere at last.

CHAPTER 10

In which Tish says goodbye

That evening, Charles did not come and get Tish for a slice of apple decorated with parsley and a glass of milk. He was too busy working on something at his desk.

Tish let himself into Charles's room. He leaned over his shoulder to see what he was making, just like he had when he was nothing but a spark. It was a list. A brand-new list. But it wasn't a list of things to do with him.

Tish stepped back and stared out the window at the city below. The curtains billowed around him. Why? he silently asked the wind. Why can't I stay here forever? Tish wondered whether it was his fault. Was it because he was too big for the swing? Too heavy for the trampoline? Too impatient for chess? Too sleepy for science class? But deep down, Tish knew it was none of those reasons. It was because of time. Charles was different now. And Tish knew he would never go back to the way he had been before. Just like the omelette Charles had made would never turn back into an egg.

Tish felt something crack inside, and wondered if his heart was just a mess of shell and egg. He didn't like time now that he knew how it could hurt him. Time wasn't fair. He wished they could go back and do everything all over again. But Charles had said that time only moved in one direction. And Charles had moved on without him.

Tish leaned in and licked Charles on the ear one last time. Then he went downstairs and let himself out the back gate. When he reached the bottom of Sprinkle Street, he turned to wave at Charles. Charles glanced up from his desk and stared out the window. But he didn't wave back. He was busy thinking. Tish could tell by the way his brow furrowed in concentration. And by the small glint

in his eye, like a speck of gold dust, Tish could tell that he had just discovered a good idea. He rumbled softly, remembering the promise that Charles had made to him on the night they first met; that he would never let him go. But over time, the promise had disappeared. The heart is a vast place, after all.

Tish tumbled through the park. Rumbled past the fountain. And stumbled over the bridge. He didn't know where he was going, but he felt the wind at his heels and knew he needed to keep moving. When he couldn't walk anymore, he tried flying: *Flap. Flap. Oh. Flap. Flap. Woe. Flap. Flap. No!*

When the sun rose, the roads and houses looked strange and unwelcoming. His legs were aching, so he looked for a place to rest. Seeing a large cherry tree and a welcoming patch of clover, he took a turn down a lane. The tree was old and full of blossoms, with branches that spread in every direction. And right in the center was a treehouse with a thin ladder made of rope hanging down beside it. Tish slumped on the grass and closed his eyes, listening to the muffled sounds of morning.

The birds sang sweetly, the breeze blew gently and the leaves rustled kindly, so that for a moment Tish almost felt at peace. It didn't stay melodious for long. A postman zipped past dinging his bell on his bicycle. A baby wailed. And doors flung open to release children who came tumbling into the street with uncombed hair and sleep in the corners of their eyes.

Tish felt a tug inside his chest. It was the first day of school holidays and they didn't want to miss a thing. Tish didn't want to miss a thing, either. He sat up straight and thumped his tail, but the girls and boys skidded and skated past him, as though he wasn't there at all. He looked down, feeling so small and alone that he thought he might disappear completely. Although he was all still there. He checked his legs and counted all of his toes. He shook his ears and his tusks. Then he gasped. His tail! What had happened to his tail?

Tish lifted up his tail. He looked at the top of it. He looked underneath it. It was covered with round purple spots. Round purple *polka dots*. He tried to rub one off, but it wouldn't budge. He tried running away from them, as fast as he could. But the polka dots came with him. The more he tried to lick or scratch or bite them off, the more of them appeared.

Afraid and confused, Tish looked for a place to hide—for a place to cry. Yet he had no place to go. Then Tish looked up at the treehouse. There was only one thing for it. And before you could say "pretty purple polka dots" three times, Tish was scrambling up the ladder.

Flap. Flap. Heave!

Flap. Flap. Ho!

Flap. Flap. Crack!

Tish was stuck halfway. His face full of bees and blossom. His brow wrinkled. The whiskers on his chin quivered. He closed his eyes, opened his jaws and,

"Ah...*tish!*"

"Bless you," said a voice.

PART 2

Elsewhere

CHAPTER 11

In which
Tish sneezes

Annabeth Arch was what some people might call a Rude Child. Annabeth didn't *think* she was rude. She just thought that she had an eye for detail, like all the greatest architects did. Was it rude to tell your mother that her nose was crooked? And your father that his load-bearing columns should be thinner? Or your teacher that she was built like a Gothic cathedral, with thick walls, round arches, and large towers, if it was true? Because of these unfortunate truths, Annabeth was often sent to The Kitchen Step. A place to Think About What She Had Done until she was Ready To Say Sorry.

The Kitchen Step was an awful place. Halfway between the kitchen and the treehouse, where all her projects and plans were out of reach. The step itself was hard and cold and damp, even on warm days. So it was, on the first day of school holidays, Annabeth was not allowed out like her brother and sisters and the kids next door but was sitting on The Kitchen Step, Thinking About What She Should Not Have Done. In particular, why she shouldn't have been sleeping on the roof. This was unfair, seeing as she had already outlined the reasons why she should: namely, because her bedroom was poorly designed, didn't have a skylight, and failed to "inspire awe" as all buildings should.

"Come on, Annabeth," called her father. "Come and apologize so you can go and find a friend to play with. You'll get mighty lonely down there."

"No, I won't," Annabeth called back, smoothing down the collar of her black turtleneck sweater. "I am never lonely. In any case, some of the greatest works of art came out of loneliness."

"No great works of art, Annabeth!" her father pleaded, remembering her last masterpiece: The

Flying Buttress. After she had innovated their toilet by adding some spires, he had been unable to sit down for a week.

Annabeth swung her legs to the side and lay down on the step to make it more ergonomic. She was planning to lie there all day, because the more that she thought about it, the less sorry she was. From her observations, having good manners was just a polite way of saying you were a very good liar and a poor observer of life. She would rather that people said what they really thought. How else would you know if your eyebrows weren't level, or if you had sawdust in your hair?

Still, a pit was growing in her stomach like the hard seeds inside the cherries that grew along the lane. She felt as though she were turning rotten, being eaten from the inside by codling moths. Although she didn't want to admit it, she *was* lonely. She had been lonely ever since she had shared some particularly unfortunate truths with her best friend, Ruby Jones, at the end of last term, namely, that Ruby Jones would never be a great gymnast like she dreamed unless she accurately measured her lines and angles. Furthermore, that she was sometimes bossy, often prissy, always competitive, and had pigtails that looked like palm trees.

Annabeth had thought she was being helpful, reasoning that *she* would like to know if she needed to work on her technique. Ruby Jones had responded by telling Annabeth she had a big mouth. Furthermore, that she was *not* an architect, so she should take off that silly black turtleneck and stop parading around like a vampire. They had not spoken since, and bowed their heads when they saw each other at gymnastics.

With nothing else to do, Annabeth fished a piece of chalk out of her pocket and sketched a picture on The Kitchen Step, the tip of her tongue sneaking out in concentration. If she didn't have a best friend anymore, perhaps she could make one? She began with a head, then a body, letting the chalk go where it wanted. It was a funny shape—sort of *beastish*. As though a mammoth, a hedgehog, a bear and a chicken had got all mixed up. Then she decorated it all over with some pretty purple polka dots. Purple polka dots were important to Annabeth Arch. After that, she gave it some pockets, since she never had enough of her own to put things in, like: her protractor, her compass, her series of plastic triangles, her sketch pad and her mechanical pencil with the 4-millimeter tip and dual-action retractor.

The step still looked gray and bare, so she drew a tree like the one out her window to give the beast some shade. When it was finished, Annabeth nodded with satisfaction. She would not be lonely. She had *made* a friend to play with. It was almost perfect. It needed a few more changes, but she could get to those later. Stretching out on the step, she lay cheek to cheek with her friend, warming the cold, hard stone. And for the first time ever, she was sorry. She was very sorry. Not for what she had said or done, exactly, but for pushing everyone so far away that they never came back. Annabeth sighed and doodled a few more polka dots on her friend's tail. Then her thoughts were interrupted by a *crack!* And something else...like a sneeze? Although it was really more like *half* a sneeze.

"Bless you," she said out of habit.

"Thank you," came a rumbly voice.

Scrambling to her feet, Annabeth stood on tiptoes and looked through the window. There was someone—or *something*—stuck in the tree and wearing a...tea cozy?

Annabeth glanced back to the living room. The coast was clear. Her parents had told her she wasn't allowed off The Kitchen Step until she had apologized, except In An Emergency and to her mind, finding a giant, woolly, rumbly beast wearing a tea cozy in your treehouse was definitely An Emergency.

CHAPTER 12

In which Tish lands on the kitchen step

Tish looked down at the girl in the black turtleneck sweater standing on the ground at the foot of the tree. Her hand on her hip. Her front teeth on her lip.

"Do you need some help?" she called.

"Yes please," Tish whimpered. His bottom hadn't been so stuck since he had tried to sit on the swings. The girl climbed up the ladder and wrapped her arms as far as she could around his waist.

"Dodecahedrons!" she puffed, wiping her brow. "You're really stuck!"

"What's a dodecahedron?" asked Tish, trying to suck in his tummy.

"It's a shape," said the girl, "with twelve flat faces."

Geometry was important to Annabeth Arch, although he didn't know that yet.

Tish winced as he looked at the ground. *One* flat face would be bad enough.

Tish turned red as the girl gave him an almighty squeeze. *Heave. Ho. Go!* He didn't budge. But he did chuckle. And chortle. And snortle. Until he was rumbling so much that he shook himself free and was halfway to the ground, hurtling towards his destiny like a falling acorn. When he finally landed with a bump on the front lawn of 6 Black Cherry Lane, damp and a little weary, the girl was gazing up at him.

"Pleased to meet you," said Tish, squinting at her through the bright sunlight.

"Oh, but we've met before," said Annabeth. "Don't you remember? It was only a moment ago. Perhaps you have a concussion."

She leaned in and checked both his eyes, lifting up his great eyelids with their long curling lashes. Her small, quick hands felt good on his face. He rumbled softly, letting off little apple-pie puffs as she inspected his ears and looked inside his jaws. Then she dug around in her pockets, pulled out a protractor and measured the angle between his ears.

"You have such great potential," she said. And while she frowned and pouted far too much for a girl of nine, her eyes were kind and glimmered with specks of gold dust.

Tish licked her on the ear. He nibbled her hair.

"Are you my Someone?" asked Tish.

"Well, I'm not just Anyone if that's what you mean!"

Their conversation was interrupted before they got to the most important parts. A man with a small crowd of children behind him came blazing through the grass towards them.

"Annabeth Arch! What do you think you're doing? You know you are not allowed off the step until you have apologized!" Her little brother poked his tongue out at her from behind his leg. And through the fence in the next-door garden, Tish saw a grubby child blowing a raspberry and waving her toy rabbit through the gaps.

"But you don't understand!" Annabeth wailed. "I was just trying to help!"

"Help who? Help *what*? You were certainly not helping anyone when you decided to sleep on the *roof*!"

"Help my...friend."

Annabeth's father looked around. He turned in a circle and rubbed his eyes, muttering something and scratching his head.

"When you *scratch* like that," said Annabeth, "you look a lot like one of the baboons I have seen at the zoo. The resemblance is *uncanny*. And a baboon is exactly the sort of pet I need in order to construct my latest project: The Greatest Bedroom In The World."

Which is how Tish found himself spending the rest of the day sitting on The Kitchen Step with Annabeth, Thinking About What She Had Done.

That night, Tish looked through Annabeth's bedroom window at his new neighborhood. The moon was full and round. He reached out to touch it, wondering whether Charles was watching that same moon. Whether he was eating his apple slices and sipping his milk. Whether he was thinking about him. Tish tried to imagine what it would be like to be Charles Dimple, although he could not. That was the

problem with being Perfect: you needed Someone to do the imagining for you. And he was with Someone new now. A long, sad sigh escaped him and the whiskers on his chin began to quiver.

"What's wrong?" asked Annabeth. "Are you sick?"

Tish shook his head, yet he did feel a little sick. *Heartsick.* And homesick. Although he knew that 33 Sprinkle Street was not his home anymore. Plus, he *had* come out in purple spots, although Annabeth had explained they were polka dots, not spots.

"It's just that I have...lost something," said Tish as he stared out the window.

"What have you lost?"

"Something special, and I don't know if I will ever find it again."

"Check your pockets," said Annabeth. "I am always finding lost things in there."

Tish blew his trunk on the curtains and wiped his eyes.

"My pockets?"

"Yes," said Annabeth, reaching down into one of his new flaps. "Extra storage is an important feature of good design."

"Oh my!" Tish said, looking side to side. "That's handy. I didn't know I had any! What's in there?"

Tish and Annabeth began emptying out his pockets onto the floor. She had put in all the usual things. There were jelly beans, golf balls, throat lozenges, a handkerchief, a pencil and a notebook, a pocket-watch, three chocolate-chip cookies, and a pair of spectacles (since from Annabeth's observations, her new friend was a touch shortsighted—she could tell by the angle of his squint).

After Tish had snapped the chocolate-chip cookie in half, he said goodnight and headed for the garden.

"Where are you going?" asked Annabeth.

"To find somewhere to sleep," said Tish.

"You don't have to sleep out there in the cold, silly. You can sleep in here with me!"

Tish beamed, his tail thumping on the floor. "May I?"

"Of course! This is your home. This is your bedroom. Mind you, it's not The Greatest Bedroom In The World—*yet*—but it's yours. And there's always the roof if you want a skylight."

Tish sniffed Annabeth's bed and nosed his way under the covers. The bed sagged a bit in the middle, but it was warm and comfortable. And in that moment, it was the best and the greatest. Snuggling up close, Annabeth scratched him behind the ears.

"*Do you snore?*" she whispered.

"*Like an oger,*" Tish whispered back.

Annabeth giggled. "*Me too.*"

She switched off the light and closed her eyes, but she could feel Tish watching her. Batting her eyes open, she saw that he had put on his new spectacles, and was leaning so close that they were eye to eye.

"What is it?" Annabeth said.

"Sawdust," said Tish. "In your hair."

And in that moment, Annabeth Arch made a promise to Tish that she would never push him away like she had to the others. Since he clearly was The Greatest Friend In The World.

CHAPTER 13

In which Tish gets a renovation

"You need a name," said Annabeth over breakfast. "A name is very important. You can't go through life without one."

Tish agreed: a name was important. But he already *had* a name. Although he had got it by accident, it was still the most precious thing he owned. The *only* thing he owned, besides his pocket-watch. He didn't want a new one.

"Well actually," said Tish, "I already have one."

"What is it?"

Tish told her his name. Savoring the sound by rolling it around in his mouth a few times. It was

86

still just as fresh and crunchy as it was when it was brand new.

"I like it," said Annabeth. "But it's not perfect yet. It needs a few changes."

Tish didn't like the sound of this. He had seen Annabeth's sketches and didn't think he would much like to have a veranda out the front, a raincap on top, or a pet baboon.

"Will it...hurt?"

Annabeth laughed.

"No, silly. I'm just thinking of a renovation. A small extension."

Tish took a moment to consider. His name *was* rather short and he was growing. Perhaps he could try one in a different size. Although he wouldn't know where to start.

"Let's play a game," said Annabeth.

"Hide-and-seek?" suggested Tish. He had wanted to play that ever since he had seen some kids playing it in the park.

"Later," said Annabeth. "This is a name-picking game. I'm going to go through the alphabet, and you are going to tell me to stop when we reach a letter that gives you a good feeling."

Alphabetizing was important to Annabeth. It was how she had learned all her architectural terms. She recited them whenever she got nervous: "*Atrium, buttress, cupola, dormer, estrade, fanlight, gable, hip roof, intrados, jetty, keystone, lintel, mortise, niche, oculus, portico, quoin, rotunda, sidelight, transom, undercroft, vault, wing wall, X-bracing, yurt...*"

Although she still couldn't decide what she preferred for the letter "Z": zaguan or ziggurat.

Tish thought that this sounded like a good idea, so they went through the alphabet from the beginning, letter by letter. Then they went back the other way. Immediately, it was clear that Tish seemed to like the letter "B" best. So they thought of all the names that they could beginning with "B." He didn't mind Bruno, Boris, Barney, Bruce, Buzz, Buddy, Buster, Benjamin, Boswell, or Benedict. He even quite liked Beowulf, but didn't feel that he could carry it off with the sort of confidence that one called Beowulf would need. But none of them were right. And every time they passed by the letter "T," Tish felt his heart hurt, since he knew it was where he truly belonged.

"How about Bert?" asked Annabeth.

"*Bert*," said Tish. He rolled it around his mouth, pressing out the creases and smoothing down the edges. It felt good. "*Bert.*"

"And that leaves you with two options for short," said Annabeth. "Because you can have Bert, or you can have Tish. Just like I can have Anna or I can have Beth depending on what day of the week it is."

Tish sat up straighter and rumbled with pride. With his name a little longer, he grew a little taller. It felt a bit stiff to start with, but he soon wore it in. He went by Bert every Friday, and Tish on all the other days. And in truth, he only ever wore the long name when it was cold and he needed a little extra padding. So, everything went on in much the same way.

CHAPTER 14

In which Tishbert has a haircut

With Tish by her side, Annabeth was spending less time on The Kitchen Step and more time doing the things she wanted to do. Like working on her projects, drawing up plans, and writing letters to her friend, Ruby Jones, although she never *sent* the letters, only kept them under her bed. Perhaps this improvement was because she had Tish to provide a second opinion. From her observations, all the greatest architects valued second opinions and saw the benefits of collaborating with a team.

"Was that rude of me back there?" she would ask Tish when they left the dentist or the post office or the supermarket. "Did I say something wrong?"

"Perhaps you could try it like this?" Tish would suggest, once the color had returned to his cheeks and his bristles had lain back flat. Yet despite Annabeth's discovery that she could make some of her unfortunate truths slightly less unfortunate if she really tried, she never withheld the truth from Tish. She was always honest and sometimes the outcome was unfortunate indeed. Like the time that she gave Tish a haircut. Or was it Bert?

"Ten, nine, eight, seven, six, five, four, three, two, one," said Bert (it being Friday). "Ready or not, here I come!" Annabeth's bedroom was still and silent.

Bert plodded around, lifting up blankets, looking into boxes and opening cupboard doors. When he couldn't find her in the bedroom, he looked in the hall, in the bathroom and in the kitchen. He had almost given up when he found Annabeth sitting on The Kitchen Step.

"Annabeth!" he said. "What are you doing here? Aren't you supposed to be hiding?"

"Sorry," said Annabeth. "I wanted to tell you but I got stuck here. I was hiding when I got myself into a...situation."

"What happened?"

"Well," said Annabeth, biting on her fingernails. "I was hiding in the treehouse when the little girl next door threw her toy rabbit over the fence. I thought it would make good stuffing for one of my new ethically designed cushions made from one hundred per cent recyclable materials, so...I took it."

Bert nodded. Ethical design was important to Annabeth Arch.

"Anyway..." Annabeth groaned and rolled her eyes, "she started crying and I told her when she cries like that, it makes her face look like one of those horrible little weasels on the back of the cereal box and I might have to use a weasel for one of my cushions if I couldn't recycle her rabbit, and she wouldn't want to be responsible for the death of a perfectly innocent weasel in the name of a cushion now, would she? Well, long story short, I gave back the rabbit, and Mom sent me here. It's completely unfair: I was just being morally creative. The whole situation is unfortunate."

"Unfortunate indeed," agreed Bert, squeezing beside her, shedding fur and feathers all over the step. The chalk picture she had drawn of him was still there. It made him rumble every time he saw it.

They were sitting there together, talking about rabbits and weasels, cereal boxes and cushions, when Bert noticed Annabeth was leaning close and *inspecting* him as though looking for cracks in a glass.

"What is it?" he asked, wondering if he had parsley in his teeth or sawdust in his fur.

"Bert," she said, "you are very hairy."

"I am," said Bert proudly.

"Have you ever wondered what you would look like without so much hair?"

"*Without* so much hair? Whatever for?"

After Annabeth had apologized for being "morally creative/ terrorizing the neighbor," she led Bert to her dressing table.

"Would you like to sit on the floor and watch while I come up with a new design?" she invited him. After a few moments of poking and prodding,

she fished around in his pockets until she found a comb and some rubber bands. She pulled and stretched and tugged at his knots with the comb, until the tufts on top of his head sat smoothly against his forehead.

"Ouch!" cried Bert.

"Sorry!" Yet it was clear from the way that she pouted and frowned that Annabeth was not finished.

Next, Annabeth tried braiding his forelock and pulled the rest of his hair into two pigtails, causing them to sit on the top of his head like two palm trees. Inspecting his chin, she plucked and tweezed his whiskers. Filed and shaped his tusks. Tied some knots in his tail so that it wouldn't drag on the ground so much. And before he could find the words to tell her that he wanted her to stop: *snip!* Annabeth had whisked out her scissors and had cut off a lock of his hair. All the way along his neck and sides she went. Snipping and trimming. Down his legs, across his chest, beneath his belly, around his wings. Until there was hardly any fur, feathers or bristles left. Only raw, sagging skin, covered in purple polka dots. Bert stared at his reflection in the mirror. His eyes burned. His chin wobbled.

"There you are!" said Annabeth.

"Here I am," mumbled Bert.

"Now you are *almost-nearly* perfect!"

"Thank you?" said Bert, feeling confused. Because hadn't he been perfect already? Just the way he was? He was of the Perfect kind, after all. And he had always been perfect to Charles Dimple. There was nothing *almost-nearly* about it. A small, spiky thought began to grow like a weed in a patch of his mind: Annabeth Arch was not just Anyone, she was his Someone. But the question was: was he hers?

CHAPTER 15

In which Tishbert finds a hobby

"What do you want to do today?" Annabeth asked Tish one morning. Soon she would be going back to school and their long days of doing nothing together would be different.

"What about going to the –?"

"Maybe later," said Annabeth before he could finish, because she wasn't really asking.

"I thought we could find you a hobby."

"What's a hobby?"

"Its something you like to do just for the fun of doing it."

He seemed to be doing a lot of things all the time. To be honest, he wasn't sure if he liked them or not. Or if he was having fun. He had never really thought about it. He couldn't imagine things any other way.

"Where do you get a hobby?" asked Tish.

"You just sort of find them, or they find you."

Tish jumped up and narrowed his eyes, looking behind him. He wasn't sure he liked the sound of something following him, sneaking up on him through the grass.

"There are lots of different kinds. Maybe you could learn an instrument or how to speak a new language. You could play a sport, or start a collection."

"Oh," said Tish, stretching out his tail. "Then I already *have* a hobby, since I have been collecting things all week. Look!"

Tish pointed to the spiky tufts on his tail. It was full of creepy crawlies. He thumped it a few times, sending his new friends scurrying through their forest of fur.

"Dodecahedrons!" Annabeth yelped, and got out her magnifying glass. It was true: he did have quite a collection. There were all sorts of bugs living in there.

"Tishbert," said Annabeth (it being a coolish day), "you're coming with me."

♥

Tish spent the day cross-legged on the bathroom floor while Annabeth combed out the bugs, listening as she told him about other things he could have as a hobby, now that his collection had been disposed of. Tish had no idea where to start figuring out what he might like to do. So, he made a list. Charles had taught him a list was a good place to start when you were trying to trap an idea.

So far, in alphabetical order, Tish had written: archery and acrobatics, beekeeping and bonsai growing, crosswords and calligraphy, dominoes and decoupage, embroidery and etching, fruit picking and flower pressing, gardening and golfing, horse-riding and hiking, ice-skating and ikebana, jigsaw puzzles and juggling, kite flying and karate, lion-taming and leaf collecting, magic tricks and martial arts, noodling and needlepoint, origami and orienteering, puppetry and picnicking, quilting and quizzes, racquetball and reading, stamp collecting and scrapbooking, tap dancing and table tennis, unicycling and underwater photography, ventriloquism and video games, whale watching and whittling, xylophoning and X-ray art, yo-yoing and yoga, ziplining and zoology.

"I nearly forgot," said Annabeth, after taking a breath. "There's also fishing, fencing, knitting, journaling, jousting, jewelry making, pottery, singing..."

Tish closed his eyes, his head spinning as Annabeth's words wove into one long, tangled piece of string. He was having trouble keeping up and he was unsure whether the butterflies fluttering around in his belly were excited or afraid. The world was even bigger and more baffling than he thought was possible. There was so much to do, and he wanted to do it all. To meet everyone. To see everything. Tish read over his list.

Once again, he seemed to be the most comfortable with the letter "B." There were lots of hobbies he liked the sound of in there: ballooning and baking. Bowling and book club and beachcombing. But one thing in particular sparked his interest.

"What about bird watching?"

He was afraid of pretend birds that he had seen—like the cuckoo clock and the rubber duck—but the real ones in the trees along Sprinkle Street had been his greatest comfort on those cold, quiet nights outside. He had seen them in all the colors of the rainbow, and listened to them each with their own sweet song. And he had admired their graceful wings that were so different to his. From what he had learned from the museum, many of them were endangered, too. On the brink of becoming extinct. He would like to see them while he still could. It being only a matter of time for them both.

"Bird watching?" Annabeth wrinkled her nose and waved off the idea as though it were a fly. Then, "I know!" she said. "What about gymnastics?"

"Gymnastics?" said Tish. "What's that?"

CHAPTER 16

In which Tishbert does gymnastics

It is safe to say that Tish did *not* enjoy his first attempt at gymnastics. For one, he found that his tail was not the least bit suited to doing handstands or cartwheels. It got all tangled up.

Annabeth, on the other hand, seemed to be enjoying it immensely. He could tell by the way her frown was only twice its usual size.

"Let's start with some stretches," said Annabeth.

Tish stretched high. Tish stretched low. Thinking all the while that if this was gymnastics, then he didn't mind it one bit. Although Annabeth was only just getting started. Next was the balance beam—in the form of a long line of stepping stones that wound through the garden.

"Look up! Straight ahead!" tutored Annabeth as she pointed her toes and held out her arms. "Don't look down."

"Like this?" Tish wobbled from side to side, but he made it along the balance beam without toppling over.

"Now for the high bar!"

Tish looked around. He couldn't see a high bar anywhere. Then he saw Annabeth heading to the cherry tree. She rubbed some dirt on her hands, hoisted herself up the trunk then swung from a branch as though it were a steel rail. Standing beneath her, Tish discovered that the cherry tree worked far better as a scratching post than for any other exercise. He was getting tired already, but Annabeth was only warming up.

Vaulting onto the ground, she led Tish to the highest place in the back garden, a grassy rise covered with clover.

Tish thought that it would be a good place to stop and have a picnic, but Annabeth had other plans in mind.

"Somersaults!" she whooped.

Tish gawked as she tucked her chin to her chest and rolled head over bottom down the hill. "Ack!" he said, feeling a small pang in his chest as the word escaped him, reminding him of Charles Dimple. Annabeth tumbled all the way to the bottom of the hill, ran back to the top and did it all over again. Then it was Tish's turn.

"Tuck your chin to your chest!" yelled Annabeth. Tish tried tucking his chin to his chest, but his tusks got in the way. *Flap. Flap. Whee. Flap. Flap. Whoa. Flap. Flap. Ouch!* Tish landed at the bottom of the hill with a whump.

"What about rhythmic gymnastics?" said Annabeth, coming over and brushing him off.

"That might be a better fit." Tish pulled a stick out of his tail. He didn't know what rhythmic gymnastics was, but he was certain that anything would be better than somersaulting down a hill. Annabeth ran inside, returning moments later with a ball, a long silk ribbon on a stick and a purple hoop.

"From my observations," she said, standing on the flat and kicking off her shoes, "gymnastics requires strength, flexibility and coordination."

Tish wasn't sure if he had any of those things, although he did have a very sore bottom. His tummy hurt. His legs hurt. His shoulders, back and chest hurt. Even his wings felt bent out of shape. Then Tish felt the pain melt away as Annabeth began her performance.

"You have to do the music," she said. So, Tish hummed a tune and thumped his tail.

Finding the rhythm, Annabeth took a deep breath before running and leaping so high that it took Tish's breath away for a moment. She rolled the ball along the ground then picked it up and danced with it as though it were alive. She made shapes and patterns with the ribbon so quickly that Tish couldn't see where Annabeth began and the ribbon ended.

"Oh!" Tish cooed. "Ah!" he sighed as Annabeth fluttered and twirled around the garden like a butterfly. Grabbing the hoop, she spun it around one arm and rolled it to the other before shimmying inside and letting it circle up and down her body with her eyes closed. Tish followed the hoop around and around with his eyes until he was spinning too. When she was finished, he stamped

his feet on the ground and raised his trunk. "Encore! Encore!"

Annabeth bowed and batted her eyelids open. Although she did not smile, Tish could tell she was proud by how straight she was standing.

"Who taught you how to do *that*?"

"Ruby Jones," said Annabeth, her head drooping. "We used to practice when she came over for a sleepover."

"Maybe she could teach me, too."

"I don't think so," said Annabeth, a familiar shadow falling across her face. Striding over, she passed the hoop to Tish. "Your turn. I will do the music."

Tish scrambled to his feet and wandered into the middle of the yard. He waited while Annabeth counted him in.

Tish began by balancing the ball on his nose. *Flap. Flap. One. Flap. Flap. Two. Flap. Flap. Pop!*

"Never mind," called Annabeth. "Keep going!"

So Tish kept going. He held the ribbon on a stick between his teeth. *Flap. Flap. Three. Flap. Flap. Four. Flap. Flap. Rip!*

"That's all right," said Annabeth, a little less

enthusiastically than before, but she still sang to encourage him.

Tish stepped into the hoop. *Flap. Flap. Five. Flap. Flap. Six. Flap. Flap. Crack!*

Annabeth went silent. She marched over and pulled the crushed hoop out from under Tish's foot.

"Sorry!" wailed Tish, his bottom lip wobbling.

Annabeth didn't stretch the truth just that little bit further as Charles would have. She snapped it across his face like an elastic band. "You are doing everything all wrong, Tishbert!"

Tish stared at his toes, his spirits deflating like the punctured ball that slumped beside him. He knew he was doing everything all wrong. He had broken her purple hoop, after all.

But something told him that it wasn't about that. That it wasn't just that he had been doing it wrong. But it was because he wasn't doing it the way that Ruby Jones did it. He watched as Annabeth packed up the equipment and stormed inside.

When Tish came inside, he found Annabeth sitting on The Kitchen Step. Her head drooped. Her shoulders slumped.

"What happened?"

"Nothing," said Annabeth, pouting firmly. "I just told the truth."

"To whom?"

Annabeth looked over her shoulder. "*Everyone.*"

Tish glanced into the living room. Annabeth's brother was sobbing. Her father was pale. Her mother was silent. Everyone at 6 Black Cherry Lane was unhappy. Especially Annabeth.

Tish flopped down beside her on the step. He nibbled Annabeth's hair. He licked her on the ear. And just like that the shadow lifted from Annabeth's face. She *almost-nearly* laughed.

They sat together in silence. Listening. Watching. A pair of finches landed on the fence. Or were they sparrows? Or wrens? Tish wanted to know. He wondered if they could see him. Tish listened to their chirrups and watched as they bobbed their heads and pecked at bugs. He was not the least bit afraid of them.

The Kitchen Step was quiet and still. It was the perfect spot for bird watching. And somewhere inside, Tish had a feeling he might be better at bird watching than he was at gymnastics. It was a warm, cozy feeling, making the top of his head all tingly right between the ears. He *almost-nearly* told Annabeth. But he kept his tusks shut, since not disappointing Annabeth Arch was important to Tish.

CHAPTER 17

In which Tishbert goes to a party

In the final week of school holidays, Tish found a letter in the mailbox. It was addressed to Annabeth Arch. Annabeth was sitting on The Kitchen Step doodling with chalk, having made three people cry before breakfast after sharing some unfortunate truths. Tish handed her the letter and put on his spectacles. It was an invitation to a birthday party at the bowling alley on Friday.

The invitation came as a surprise, since Annabeth did not receive many invitations.

But what was more surprising, was the fact that it was an invitation to Ruby Jones's birthday party.

Ruby Jones, who Annabeth had not spoken to for weeks. *Ruby Jones*, who Annabeth said she would never talk to again.

Tish was excited. He had never been bowling before. He had never been to a birthday party.

Annabeth was not excited. She stuffed the invitation into her pocket and announced that she Would. Not. Go.

However, when the day of the party arrived, Tish found Annabeth dressed and wrapping a present at the kitchen table. Tish recognized what was in the parcel immediately; it was the thick pile of letters Annabeth had been writing to Ruby Jones and hiding under her bed. He also recognized that Annabeth was nervous by the number of unfortunate truths that she was sharing. He had noticed that the more Annabeth had on her mind, the harsher she became.

"Bert," she said (it being Friday), "You are very smelly."

"I am," said Tish proudly. It was on account of his haircut. For while his coat had *almost-nearly* grown back, it was not as soft and comfortable as it had once been. It was itchy and patchy, and Tish had taken to rolling in whatever he could to scratch the parts he couldn't reach.

"And when was the last time you brushed your tusks?" she asked, pinching her nose.

Tish opened his jaws as she stood on a chair and tossed in a breath mint. Then she pulled a brush out of her pocket and fussed about with his hair, piling it up in bunches on the sides again, making his head look like an island with two palm trees sticking out of it. Around each tree, she tied a purple polka dot ribbon. He could tell she was nervous by the way she was practicing quietly as she combed his hair: "*Atrium, buttress, cupola, dormer, estrade, fanlight, gable, hip roof, intrados, jetty, keystone, lintel, mortise, niche, oculus, portico, quoin, rotunda, sidelight, transom, undercroft, vault, wing wall, X-bracing, yurt...*"

She stopped as she always did when she got to "Z."

Tish felt nervous too. He had thought birthday parties were supposed to be fun, but now he wasn't so sure.

"Done!" said Annabeth, spinning Tish around to see in the mirror.

Tish stared back as his reflection and was faced with an unfortunate truth: he hardly recognized himself.

As they left the house, Tish took his old umbrella off the hook at the front door, tucking it under his trunk for comfort. But Annabeth prized it away and hung it back on the hook.

"It's not going to rain," she said. "Why do you have this old thing, anyway?"

Tish gazed at his umbrella, fighting the urge to snatch it back. He wanted to tell her the truth—that he had it for one reason only: because umbrellas were important to Charles Dimple. And things that were important to Charles Dimple were important to him. He had discovered this one afternoon while daydreaming in a patch of clover, nibbling on a clod of dirt: this was what happened when you loved Someone. It had happened with Annabeth too: purple polka dots were important to him now, alongside all the other things that were important to Annabeth.

Tish mumbled something about it looking stormy out and how the weather seemed to be changing. Because he wasn't sure that Annabeth would understand. She always said she wanted to be told the truth, but sometimes it seemed that the truth wasn't what she really wanted to hear.

Tish followed Annabeth down Black Cherry Lane and around the block to the shops. Cutting through a field, they reached a series of squat, yellowing buildings that sat in the middle of a cement square like giant blocks of cheese. Which reminded Tish that it was nearly lunchtime. He wouldn't mind some cheese. And maybe even some crackers.

Inside, the bowling alley was loud and bright. Lights flashed. Pins cracked. Machines pinged. And silhouettes cheered. There were balloons floating on the ceiling and a disco ball sending silver moonbeams across the dance floor.

Annabeth hung close to Tish as they waded through strangers, carving a path to the place where kids stood in clusters like a bunch of cornflake cakes and chocolate treats. Tish thumped his tail in time to the music and glanced around. Nobody except Annabeth could see him, yet he felt shy all the same. He kept his eyes peeled for the flick of a tail or the curve of a spike. Yet there were no

Perfects at the party. Each child's imagination sat wrapped up and waiting like the presents piled in the corner. Tish sighed and shuffled a bit to the music. If it wasn't for the table piled with food waiting untouched in the corner, Tish might have decided he didn't like parties.

As Tish approached the table, his trunk began to quiver at the scent of something delicious. There were bowls of fruit salad and popcorn. Wheels of cheese and crackers. Tiny pastries. Jello cups. Wooden skewers stacked with marshmallows and chocolate-dipped strawberries. And in the very center of the table stood a cake topped with a tiny figurine of a gymnast twirling in the icing. Tish honed in on what smelled so delicious. Inside a bowl were small and green nuts, sitting in their shells like salty, hidden jewels.

"Pistachios!" trumpeted Tish.

"Yuck!" said Annabeth, seeing Tish reaching his trunk towards the bowl.

"Stay away from those—you won't like them. Besides, they are so poorly designed—they take too long to open and are tiny. All that work for nothing."

Tish stepped back from the bowl, although his

mouth watered and his stomach growled. He let out a small puff and munched on an egg and lettuce sandwich instead.

When he had worked his way through half a wheel of cheese and polished off the crackers, he noticed Annabeth was smiling, her face lit up like candles on a cake. Following her gaze across the dance floor, he searched for what it was that had transformed his Someone. And he found it. She was smiling at Someone Else. A girl with hair piled up in bunches on the sides, making her head look like an island with two palm trees sticking out of it. And wrapped around each tree was a purple polka dot ribbon. The girl smiled back. Tish knew who she was, but asked anyway, just to make sure.

"Is that Ruby Jones?"

"I'll be back in a minute," Annabeth called to Tish.

"Ok," said Tish. "I'll wait here."

Then Tish saw something that he would never forget: Annabeth running, stumbling, *skidding* across the dance floor as she made her way to Ruby Jones. Then Annabeth was laughing. Not *almost-nearly* laughing but truly laughing, from her eyes all the way to her belly. And Ruby Jones was laughing. They were both laughing and laughing. And Tish could tell that Ruby Jones was laughing not only because it was her birthday. But because Annabeth Arch was there. Annabeth Arch: her perfectly imperfect friend.

Now Tish knew why purple polka dots were important to Annabeth. Because purple polka dots were important to Ruby Jones. No one was more important than Ruby Jones. And whatever Annabeth and Ruby Jones had imagined had happened between them was not important anymore. That was the truth, no matter how you looked at it.

CHAPTER 18

In which Tishbert hears a whisper

By the time Tish had eaten his way through most of the food, watched five games of bowling and counted every balloon in the room, Annabeth had still not come back to get him. His head felt heavy and his eyelids drooped. Finding a quiet place, Tish yawned and pawed at the carpet, turned in a few circles and lay down on the ground while he waited for Annabeth. He hadn't planned to fall asleep, but when he woke up, the room was empty. The lights were off. The disco ball had stopped spinning. The party was over.

"Annabeth?" Tish called. "Are you there?"

His voice echoed around the room and came bouncing back.

Tish sat on his haunches and waited for Annabeth to come and get him. The bowling alley was strewn with streamers and colored bits of paper. There were still a few crumbs of birthday cake left, although he had lost his appetite. He swept them away with his tail and tried not to worry. Then he brightened. I know, he thought, she's playing a game. Games were something that happened at parties. It's a game of hide and seek! She is probably waiting for me to find her.

Tish went outside. He counted backwards from ten, then stumped through the field outside the bowling alley calling, "Ready or not, here I come!" The field was empty, and the streets looked all but deserted.

Tish sat in the dirt. A storm rumbled in the distance sending a dark thought sweeping through his mind like a black cloud. It cast a shadow over his heart and whispered something. Tish tried not to listen, but he heard the whisper again, *Maybe...*

"Maybe what?" said Tish, unable to ignore it. A familiar icy chill spread through his body.

"*Maybe she has forgotten you.*"

Tish waved it away, since it would be very rude of Annabeth to forget him and, in Tish's opinion, despite what anybody else thought, Annabeth Arch was not a Rude Child. She was also not a Late Child. Or a Forgetful Child. She was not in the habit of forgetting Important Things or disappearing.

Tish thought of something else. It was a bad something. A dark and stormy something. And the something was this: Annabeth Arch was in grave danger. Annabeth Arch needed help.

"Something has happened to her!" he said, scrambling to his feet. "A bad something!"

It began to rain, and for the first time, Tish did not have his umbrella with him. There was a crack and a roar. The storm had arrived. And it was too late for him to go anywhere. Tish stood tall, bracing himself against the wind as the rain lashed his face.

He watched the dark clouds gather around him, stalking like hungry wolves. Sparks shot into the sky as lightning struck a distant tree. He wanted to wail and drop to his knees, but he remembered that this was why Charles had made him so BIG, after all. Big enough to hide beneath in a storm.

He felt the empty space beneath him where no one huddled. Closing his eyes, he thought about Annabeth, hoping she was safe and sound. And he thought about Charles. Wishing that wherever he was, he was warm and dry.

That both of his friends were out of the rain.

CHAPTER 19

In which Tishbert waits a minute

After the storm passed, Tish splashed his way through the neighborhood calling for Annabeth. When he had searched in every place he could think of, he sloshed down Black Cherry Lane to try and look for clues. It was cherry blossom time and the trees were thick with flowers. A small face peered through the window of the yellow house next door. A face covered with jam and springy ringlets. Tish felt his heart lift, but it was not Annabeth. Only the child who he heard crying through the night sometimes when she threw her rabbit out of bed.

Tish went on searching. He didn't have to look much further. Because as soon as he arrived at Number 6, he found who he had been looking for. His tail thumped. His heart leapt. Annabeth Arch was not in grave danger. Annabeth Arch was at home, safe and sound, perched in her treehouse. She was wearing purple polka dot pajamas and had a mouth full of popcorn. And perched beside her was Ruby Jones, who was also wearing purple polka dot pajamas and shining a flashlight through the leaves.

As relief faded it was replaced by something new. Tish's tail stopped thumping. His heart stopped leaping. And something else washed over him. It was hot and prickly and spread all the way from the tops of his toes to the tips of his tusks. He didn't like that feeling. And in that moment, he didn't much like anything at all. Curling up at the foot of the tree, Tish yawned and watched the yellow flashlight lighting up the dark sky. It was late and the day had sapped him of his energy. He fell asleep listening to the sounds of Ruby Jones's giggles as Annabeth told her a spooky ghost story. And as he listened, he wondered if he was nothing but a ghost. If anyone could see him at all.

♥

After a restless night, Tish opened one eye and watched as Ruby Jones made her way down the ladder, stepping over the top of him as though he were a bike or a shovel. His heart pounding, Tish watched Annabeth stand up and move towards him. Then something happened that Tish would never forget. Annabeth didn't step over him, she stepped on *top* of him, walking right across his back as though he were a balance beam.

"Ow!" he wailed as she trod on his tail.

"Dodecahedrons!" Annabeth jumped. "I didn't see you there."

Tish sat up and rubbed the sleep from his eyes, wondering if he was stuck in a bad dream.

"Are you coming?" called Ruby Jones from the house.

"Coming!" Annabeth waved. She turned to Tish and patted him on the head, saying, "I'll be back in a minute." She ran to catch up with Ruby Jones.

And just like that, Tish found himself waiting. Again. He waited for a minute. He waited while Annabeth and Ruby Jones had breakfast. He waited while they did somersaults down the hill, and finally saw what a somersault was *meant* to look like: Ruby Jones was very good at gymnastics. He waited while they had lunch. He waited while they drew up plans and designed The Greatest Playground In The World, and shared afternoon tea. He waited while they did chalk drawings on The Kitchen Step. He waited while Ruby Jones packed her toothbrush, her pillow and her sleeping bag and walked home.

After Ruby Jones had left, a warm, hopeful rumble started in Tish's belly. He felt sure the minute was over. Time ticked on. Tish kept waiting. He waited while Annabeth ate her dinner and dessert. He waited while she had a bath and combed her hair. He waited until it was dark. And after all the lights in the house had gone out except Annabeth's, Tish felt that feeling again; the hot, prickly feeling that spread all the way from the tops of his toes to the tips of his tusks.

Rising to his feet, Tish went looking. On his way past The Kitchen Step, he noticed that the chalk drawing of him had almost disappeared. There were only a few small traces of him left where he used to be. When he reached Annabeth's bedroom, he saw a light beneath the door. Opening the door, he saw Annabeth in bed. She didn't say a word. Her eyes were closed. Her breath was steady. Tish came closer, watching as she dreamed. He pulled the blankets over her shoulders and switched off the light.

Tish curled up beneath the cherry tree on the storm-soaked grass. The night was still and quiet except for the brief wail of the little girl next door. She had probably lost her rabbit again. He looked for a bird in the tree—for one of the owls or nightjars he had seen in Charles's encyclopedias, but he was alone. And not just on the outside, but on the inside too. Annabeth was only a few walls away, but there was a greater distance between them and in that space lay a truly unfortunate truth. Annabeth would not come looking for him again. Not after a minute. Not after a day. Not after a week. And he heard another whisper from deep within his heart that said, *What are you waiting for?*

CHAPTER 20

In which Tishbert says goodbye. Again.

Tish was right. Annabeth never did come looking. She was too busy making plans, going to school and spending time with Ruby Jones. Tish got a whole loaf smaller, his coat got a whole hand thinner, and his snores got a whole trunk softer. His wings, however, stayed the same. (He had improved at flying and a flap or two could almost get him as high as the treehouse.)

Some nights, as he gazed at the stars, he heard the whisper again. Tish didn't know how to answer the call from inside him. He was stuck halfway between two hard places. On the one tusk, he didn't want to spend his life waiting. He didn't want to be a project—a poorly made imitation of Someone Else. He didn't want to be renovated or extended or given a fresh coat of paint. But on the other tusk, he needed Someone. Someone to imagine a life for him, otherwise he would disappear just like the others had. He didn't want to become extinct. He didn't want to be put in a museum.

Tish dropped to his knees to watch a ladybug. He thought and thought. And when he returned to that small patch in his mind, the weed had grown into a vine and it was clear what he thought. Tish wasn't Annabeth's Someone. But Annabeth was not his either.

The following morning, Tish peered over the fence. He looked at the roads and hills stretching out to the horizon.

I cannot be the last, he thought. There must be another like me. Tish decided to go looking. It wouldn't be easy—his Someone could be Anywhere. Yet Tish knew it was the right decision by the way his tail felt lighter. And he felt a rumble stir in his belly again, like a rusty engine warming up.

He waited until Annabeth had finished her breakfast, then he knocked on the trunk of her treehouse. She poked her head out of the window.

"Bert," she said (it being Friday), "there you are."

She looked him up and down, smiling wide. Her hand on her hip. Her teeth on her lip, as always. He was pleased that she could see him, not like Charles, but he no longer saw the spark in her eyes—the flecks of gold dust. And he knew that he had lost something. Something special. Again.

"Have you been looking for me?" asked Tish, his tail thumping.

"No," said Annabeth. "But now you're here, could you please hold this measuring tape for me?"

Tish held the tape, trying to dislodge a lump in his throat, while Annabeth wrote down lengths and breadths. She had given up on her last project, and was working on designing The Greatest Treehouse In The World.

"I've just come to...to say goodbye."

"Oh," said Annabeth, the tape sliding back with a snap. She swung down the ladder and stood beneath him.

"Where are you going?"

"I'm not sure yet," said Tish.

"Come back and visit, won't you?" Annabeth stood on her tiptoes and gave him a squeeze around the neck.

Tish closed his eyes, blowing small apple-pie puffs against her cheek. He wanted to remember this moment and how her small, quick hands felt on his face. He waited for Annabeth to stop him—to try and convince him to stay. But she didn't. So he nibbled her hair, licked her on the ear and walked towards the gate.

"Hold on," called Annabeth.

Tish turned to her expectantly, his heart leaping. "Yes!"

"There's something you need."

Tish turned in a few circles as Annabeth disappeared. She returned with Tish's umbrella.

"Oh," said Tish, rumbling softly. Since although it wasn't what he had been expecting, or hoping, it was even better. For the first time, he knew for certain that he was important to Annabeth, since umbrellas were important to Tish. Tucking the umbrella beneath his trunk, Tish began to head off but turned, remembering he had something for her, too.

"Annabeth," he called.

"What is it?"

"I've been thinking about 'Z.' I like ziggurat best."

Annabeth murmured something under her breath, tapping out a rhythm with her foot, before grinning widely. "Me too!"

Tish watched as she climbed back up the ladder, reciting softly to herself as though it were the periodic table: "*Atrium, buttress, cupola, dormer, estrade, fanlight, gable, hip roof, intrados, jetty, keystone, lintel, mortise, niche, oculus, portico, quoin, rotunda, sidelight, transom, undercroft, vault, wing wall, X-bracing, yurt...ziggurat!*"

Tish waved goodbye. He looked around and sniffed the air.

Then he took his first step on the way to Anywhere.

PART 3

Anywhere

CHAPTER 21

In which Tishbert leaves for Ever-Never

It was the end of the cherry blossoms. The path was pink and white like a frosted cake. Tish waded through the fallen petals as though wading through fresh snow.

"You're just like me," he said to those last spring blooms. "The last of your kind."

He wondered if they were lonely. If they were afraid.

He looked around for other things that might be the last. He found the last drop of dew. The last shred of cloud. The last thread of web. Besides being last, they all had something else in common:

to most they were invisible. People looked straight through them when they passed them by.

When he came to the last house on Black Cherry Lane, he stopped. There was something on the road. Tish dropped to his knees to get a closer look. Brushing off the leaves and dirt, he saw what it was: a rabbit. Damp and limp. Unmoving. Tish nudged it, wishing it would jump up and hop away, but it was only a toy. He could tell by its ears that it had once been white, but had since been loved into a dirty gray. It was so worn and threadbare that it was close to unraveling; like Tish himself, or so he felt. As he picked it up, he knew it belonged to the child in the yellow house next door to Number 6. He had seen it countless times before, being shoved through the gaps in the fence by the little girl with bouncy ringlets and grubby feet. He knew it was her favorite—her perfect friend—since she was always dragging it around, dangling it from a window and calling for it through the night.

Tish glanced back down the lane. He couldn't leave the rabbit lying here so far from home. She would be wondering where it was. He would have to go back.

As Tish rounded the corner, he looked for the drop of dew, the shred of cloud and the thread of web. But they had all disappeared. Perhaps they are on a journey too, thought Tish.

Drawing nearer, he heard the familiar wail of the girl. Tish stepped quicker, his feet shaking the ground. She wants her rabbit! She needs her rabbit!

He didn't like that wailing sound. It was the sound of someone whose heart was breaking. Hearing it growing louder, Tish began loping as fast as he could. *Flap. Flap. Thump. Flap. Flap. Bump. Flap. Flap. Whump!* Rounding the corner, he could see the girl's tear-streaked face over the fence as she tore around the garden. She was searching in her sandpit, tearing through her cubby, tipping out flowerpots and her guinea pig's water bowl, all the while calling out, "Gone!"

At the gate, Tish took a deep breath and tossed the rabbit through the air over the hedge. It spun a few times before flopping at her feet. The girl stopped crying. She stared at the rabbit, her eyes wild with shock. She picked it up by the tail, her lip trembling.

Tish sighed with relief as she held it close. All was right and still once again. He slumped on all fours and listened to a bird singing. He wondered what it was. A robin? Or a nightingale? Then a howl pierced the silence as the girl threw the rabbit on the ground and returned to moaning. Tish wanted to howl and moan too. It was an awful sight.

Had something happened to the rabbit? Had she lost something else? Her mother rushed outside and tried to comfort her, scooping her up and rocking her from side to side.

"Shh, Izzy, shh."

"Gone!" she sobbed. "Gone for ever-never!"

"Shh, my darling, shh. Nothing is gone forever and ever."

The girl sucked desperately on her thumb, but it did not seem to help, having given that habit away weeks ago. She had got a new doll as a reward, although it already lay abandoned in the sandpit, its head pulled off.

"*Izzy*," whispered Tish. The name fizzed and popped on his tongue like a sherbet.

Once Izzy had exhausted herself, she flopped against the fence like a rag doll, whimpering quietly as she stared through the gaps. She had picked up her rabbit and was sucking on one of its ears. From the lane, Tish could see she was watching Annabeth in her treehouse. *Annabeth*, thought Tish. *She wants Annabeth.* Tish stepped closer, wondering if he should go back and call out to Annabeth, or find her brother and sister for Izzy to play with. But Izzy had stopped crying. She stood up. She was looking at Tish. Then Izzy was stumbling over her two small feet in her too big shoes, moving closer and closer.

Izzy had not been looking for her rabbit—although she was very pleased to have it back. She had been looking for Tish. Or was it Bert?

"Bertie!" she squealed, having found her own name halfway in between. She giggled and wrapped her arms around Bertie's leg. Her cheeks were sticky and her yellow ringlets bounced around her round face like sunbeams. Grabbing him by the tail, Izzy pulled him through the hedge and into her garden.

Bertie's mind struggled to catch up with his tail as she led him under trees and into the sandpit. How had this happened? He hadn't gotten Anywhere. And yet, here he was.

When they reached the yellow house, Tish leaned down and looked into Izzy's eyes. A bright spark flickered inside them, glimmering with specks of gold dust. And she did not look straight through him, but *at* him, right into the very core of him. He was not invisible to her. And he could see that this was not the first time she had seen him, that she had been watching and waiting for a long time. That her heart had been calling out for him to play with her ever since he had arrived. She wasn't ready for him to leave. She didn't want him to go Anywhere.

"Not gone?" she asked, a sob catching in her throat.

"Not gone," said Bertie, licking away her tears. She smelled like hot buttered bread with jam. "Hello."

CHAPTER 22

In which Bertie
goes sailing

Isabella Applebee was known as Izzy for short. She was short, too, as most three-year-olds tend to be. And she only ever wore her name long when she was in trouble. Like when she jumped on the bed, or got into the bath with all her clothes on, or ate all the strawberries on the way home from the shops. Izzy liked shouting, cookies, pirates, her guinea pig, Bob, dressing up, crying and laughing at the same time, and pretending to eat her dinner like a dog: on all fours, with only her tongue. But she didn't like sleeping much—not at the usual times at least—as Bertie was about to discover.

"Wakey time," said a voice in Bertie's ear.

A finger was gouging open Bertie's left eye, lifting up the lid and looking inside. He batted his eyes open and saw Izzy's face up close, although his right eye stayed dark. Perhaps it's still night time over on the right, he thought. Closing both his eyes, he tucked his tail in close and went back to sleep. Izzy's bedroom was small but cozy, and he hadn't had such a good night's sleep in ages.

"*Grum, grum, grum*," he rumbled. Then a loud noise sent him scrambling to his feet.

"Wakey tiiiiiime!"

Propping himself up, Bertie peeped through one eye and saw something looking back at him in the mirror on the wall. A sort of *pirate*. Bertie leaned in towards his reflection. He had an eye-patch over his right eye, a hat on his head, and a golden ring dangling from one of his ears. Beside him, Izzy was hunting through her dress-up box, burbling to a stuffed parrot on her shoulder. A wary-looking guinea pig was propped on a pillow wearing a tutu. Guinea pigs were important to Isabella Applebee.

Bertie looked around. It turned out it wasn't night time, not here anyway, although it felt like

night time since it was so early in the morning. He longed to go back to sleep, but it didn't seem as though he had any say in the matter.

"Pretend I'm a pirate and you're a pirate and I have a parrot but you don't and we're on a boat and there are crocodiles."

Bertie tried, but he couldn't really, since he didn't have an imagination. He mumbled something piratey about being careful not to wake the crocodiles.

"Not like *that*," Izzy groaned and dragged Bertie out of bed by his tail. "Like this." She made a fierce face and peered at him through her toilet roll binoculars. "Go away, you bad crocodiles. You're baddies and we're baddies too!"

"Dodecahedrons!" yelped Bertie, feeling a sharp pang as he thought of Annabeth.

"Scrub the deck!" Izzy ordered.

"Oh," said Bertie. He thumped the ground with his tail.

"No, do it like this: 'Aye aye, Captain!'"

"Aye aye, Captain," said Bertie.

"No, do it like this: 'Aye aye, Captain!'"

"Aye aye, Captain," said Bertie.

"No, do it like this: 'Aye aye, Captain!'"

"Aye aye, Captain!" trumpeted Bertie, raising his trunk in a salute.

"Yarrrr!" Izzy bellowed. "Say 'yarrrrrrrrr' like this."

"Yarrrrrrrrrr!" called Bertie.

"No, do it like this: 'yarrrrrrrr!' Say 'yarrrrrrrr' like this.

"'Yarrrrrrrrrr!'" copied Bertie, just as Izzy had done.

"No, do it like this: 'yarrrrrrrr!' Say 'yarrrrrrrr' like this."

"Yaaaaaaaaaaaarrrrrrrrrrrrrrrrrrrrrr!" bellowed Bertie until the room shook and Bob scurried under the bed. Izzy nodded. She got out some string and started tying up her stuffed parrot. Bertie dropped to his knees and got to work scrubbing the deck.

Bertie and Izzy spent the morning on the high seas, searching for land and buried treasure. But Bertie got seasick and the game ended swiftly when he tried to walk the plank and broke it: *crack!*

After that, it was face painting and pasting, pulling and pinching and decorating Bertie's tail. By the end, Bertie was so covered in glitter and glue that it made him sneeze, "*Ah-tish-oo!*," sending a dazzling cloud swirling through the room. When Izzy was sent outside for morning tea, Bertie sat in the sandpit looking for birds. Izzy circled around him on her tricycle, singing a song and crunching on something. She pedaled over and held out her hand. Bertie stooped down to see what was in it. Clutched in her fingers were a few raisins, a half-eaten crust and something else. He sniffed it. It smelled salty and sweet. Bertie's whiskers quivered. His mouth watered.

"Want some?" Izzy asked. "They're stachios."

Bertie was just about to say yes, thank you. That he couldn't think of anything that he would like to eat more than pistachios, when she pedaled off. He had taken too long to answer and she was not in the habit of waiting. Bertie tried not to cry as he watched her pop the last nut into her mouth. But he was so hungry, and it is hard not to cry when you are hungry.

Bob, the guinea pig, was not the least bit sympathetic. He sniffed around, trying to find the last of the crumbs, dug a hole, and squatted down, marking his territory right where Bertie was sitting.

It was as though Bob couldn't see him at all. Or if he could, that he would rather Bertie *had* gone for ever-never.

Bertie sighed and looked over the fence. Annabeth and Ruby Jones were eating their own morning tea in the treehouse. The treehouse looked different. It had new shutters and windows and a contraption on the roof. Bertie recognized the design from one of Annabeth's sketches and beamed, since in Bertie's opinion, despite what anybody else thought, Annabeth Arch was not a Rude Child.

Annabeth Arch was The Greatest Architect In The World.

CHAPTER 23

In which Bertie goes to nursery school

Fortunately, Bertie didn't stay hungry for long. As while Izzy spent most of her day asking for snacks, when it came to breakfast, lunch or dinner, she didn't want a spoon of it, unless she had mashed it together into a ball or it was shaped into some sort of face. And when she found that her tomatoes had not been used for eyes, that her carrot had not been used for a nose, and that her bread had not been made into a happy face, she pushed it aside and gave the whole plate to Bertie. In between meals, Bertie followed her around like a vacuum cleaner, sucking up the scraps behind her. "*Grum, grum, grum.*"

The days Izzy went to nursery school were even better, since not only could Bertie have his pick from her lunchbox, but he was also able to collect all the scraps left behind by all the other children. There was always the odd orange quarter tossed beneath the flying fox. Or slice of cheese on the slide. Once he even found a blueberry muffin in the toilets. It was not *in* the toilet, mind you, but on the sink in a paper bag. Yet the best part of the day was when he got to walk alongside Izzy on the way to classes, her pink-and-purple school bag hooked to a tusk.

Every morning, Bertie kept his eyes peeled for the flick of a tail or the curve of a spike. He never saw one. And he wasn't sure whether or not the other children could see him, since they ran so fast and screeched so loudly that he could hardly hear himself think. Yet despite the noise and mess—despite the globs of cake batter he found in his ears, and the knots that were tied in his tail—Bertie enjoyed his days with Izzy. He was growing stronger every moment.

♥

"Why do you have that?" asked Izzy when she was getting dressed one morning. (And by dressed, I mean she had been told to get dressed forty-five minutes ago, yet had still only managed to put on one sock, twelve hair clips and a bathing suit, although she was not going swimming.)

Bertie was still in bed. He had been watching birds out the window. There was one that had a song like a harp but better. It was as though it had strings inside its wings, the notes gliding up and down as it flew.

"Why do I have what?" asked Bertie, checking that he had not wet the bed again.

"That thing in your hair. That nest."

"A *nest*?" said Bertie, scrambling out of bed to get a look in the mirror.

Izzy was right. There was a nest growing out the top of his head.

"How ever did that get there?" asked Bertie, turning his head from side to side. He could hardly see it. Yet he could *feel* it. It was only tiny and sat in the new tufty bits halfway between his ears.

It was not a nest made of sticks and dirt. It was not something that needed to be combed or pulled out. It was a part of him. A small, woven bed made of fresh feathers and down, growing and alive. The nest was empty.

Although, Izzy had just about lost interest and would forget about it by breakfast.

"Pretend," said Izzy, "my bed is a nest and you are in the nest and you are a bird but you are the baby and I am the mother and you eat worms."

CHAPTER 24

In which a mysterious something happens

One bright afternoon, Bertie found Izzy frowning and whining in the sandpit. She was wearing that particular expression unique to her: the perfect mix of sweet and sour, so you never knew whether to laugh and tickle her, or tell her to pick up her sandwich from the floor, take the guinea pig out of the bath, and stop complaining for Pete's *sake*!

"*Dad-eeeee*," she pleaded with her father through the window. "*Puh-lease* can I have a horsey ride?"

She had already had *two* horsey rides, plus a camel, moose and whale ride. Mr. Applebee had spent most of his morning on his hands and knees. Bertie could tell from the muddy patches on his trousers. But now Mr. Applebee was doing errands inside and recovering.

Although Izzy was only small, she had strong, relentless legs that liked to kick and gouge you right in the ribs as she galloped you around the garden.

"Why don't you play with Bob? Give him a brush, or clean out his hutch?" called her father.

Bob huffled and snuffled, and stared straight through them both as usual. He had always ignored Bertie, but he had been ignoring Izzy since yesterday too, when she painted his nose with blueberry yogurt and called him Bob-berry for the day. Bob-berry being a very undignified and childish sort of name for a guinea pig of his age and status.

"But I can't ride Bob!" she wailed, although for a moment you could tell she was considering it.

Then Bertie had an idea. "I can take you for a ride?"

He was not a horse, but he was as fast as a Thoroughbred, as feathery as a Clydesdale, as fluffy as a Shetland and could eat *three times* as many carrots. Izzy beamed and trotted over, wiping the tears from her face. "Crocodile Tears," her parents called them. But Bertie didn't think she looked one bit like a crocodile, although she could be every bit as snappy.

Dropping to his knees, Bertie bowed his head and waved his trunk, signalling for Izzy to hop on. Izzy giggled and climbed onto his back. She grabbed a large tuft of hair at the base of his neck and squeezed him tight. Her strong little legs and warm breath against his neck felt good.

"Giddy up!" she squealed and snorted, giddy herself with excitement.

Bertie began walking around the garden, treading gently as Izzy found her balance. She moved in time with his gait and leaned into the corners as they went around the sandpit.

"Faster!" she yelled.

Bertie picked up the pace and moved into a trot, doing small circles one way and then the other, before going in a big figure eight, huffing hot apple-pie puffs into the air.

"Go, Bertie! Go! Higher, Bertie. Higher!"

Bertie went faster. Bertie stepped higher. His little wings began to buzz and hum. Working harder and harder as Izzy urged him on. *Flap. Flap. Whoosh. Flap. Flap. Swoosh. Flap. Flap. Push!*

"No, not like thaaaaat. Fly, Bertie, *fly!*"

"Where do you want to go?" asked Bertie.

"Anywhere!" squealed Izzy.

Then something happened. Something strange and mysterious. Bertie felt something shift inside him, as though he were stepping into his own power, casting off an old skin. He felt the muscles in his shoulders stretch and his wings spread wider than they had ever gone before. Then to Izzy's delight and his great astonishment, the ground gave way beneath them. His legs kicked off the ground and he *flew*. Not as he had before, but just as the birds did. Those beautiful, graceful creatures that swooped and soared.

Feeling the clouds slap his cheeks, Bertie glided up and up. Soaring over the fence. Swooping over the hills. Sailing over buildings. Heading towards the mountains. The air smelled cleaner and the clouds seemed whiter than ever before. The sky spread out before him. There were no signs or streets guiding the way, only wide-open space. Then Bertie faltered and jerked. Not knowing where to go, he began to fly back to Charles. Yet seeing Sprinkle Street from above made his feather heart feel heavy. Bertie began to sink, down and down and down. Until they came crashing to the ground with a *crack*.

Yet that wasn't the strangest part. For you see, when Bertie opened his eyes, they were back at the yellow house, heaped in a pile in Izzy's garden, having only gotten as far as the hedge. They hadn't been above the clouds, above the city. They hadn't gone Anywhere, for it had only been in his mind.

"You're my very best friend in the whole world ever, Bertie!" Izzy giggled, sliding off and twirling away with bits of sticks and leaves in her hair. Bertie beamed but stayed where he was, sitting dizzy beside the hedge, trying to catch his breath.

Something had happened—*something magical*. He just wasn't sure what.

CHAPTER 25

In which things go wobbly

"Do you have any hobbies?" Bertie asked Izzy when they were sitting in the sun one afternoon. It was hot, so Bertie was fanning them both with his large ears and flapping away the flies.

"Nope," said Izzy. Bertie could tell she wasn't really listening. She was too busy trying to peel the paper wrapper off her pink crayon.

"Something you like to do just for the fun of doing it?"

Izzy put down her crayon and thought. She had her finger firmly lodged in a nostril and was wiggling it around. So, Bertie was sure that he already knew at least *one* of her hobbies. She also liked taking one bite of fruit and then putting it back in the fruit bowl.

"I like foam," she said after she had searched the other nostril.

"What's foam?"

Izzy marched into the bathroom, dragging her rabbit along beside her, and went into the shower. She began to decorate the glass with her father's shaving cream.

"Of course," trumpeted Bertie. "Foam! I like doing that too."

Izzy started with foam spots and Bertie tried making foam stripes. Then they drew a face and Izzy practiced writing the letter "I." The letter "I" was important to Isabella Applebee. She had one on her door, one on her bag, one on her hat and one sewn into the corner of a handkerchief.

"What else do you like doing?" asked Bertie when the can of shaving cream was empty.

"Beds!" said Izzy.

"How do you play beds?" asked Bertie, hoping it had something to do with sleeping in them and

nothing at all to do with gymnastics. Sleeping being one of his very best hobbies.

Izzy took Bertie into her parents' bedroom and began to jump on their bed. Izzy's rabbit bounced and hopped.

"Oh, *beds!*" said Bertie, crossing his claws that bouncing on a bed would be different to bouncing on a trampoline. "That's one of my favorite hobbies too—I *think*."

Bertie was too big to fit on the bed next to Izzy, so he rested his head on the mattress and let her bounce it up and down. Bertie's ears flapped up and down, too. *Flap. Flap. Whee! Flap. Flap. Whoah.* Then... *Flap. Flap. Crack!*

"Oh no!" wailed Bertie. "Oh dear, oh dear, *oh dear!*"

Izzy bounced off the bed and rushed to his side. "Bertie?"

"I broke it! I broke it!" Bertie wailed.

While you might be thinking that Bertie had broken the bed, he had in fact broken a tusk. At least he *thought* he had. He hadn't really—he had just lost a tusk. A very wobbly tusk. For at this point in time, Bertie only had baby tusks. And a tusk is just a rather large tooth, or "a modified incisor tooth" as Charles Dimple would say. So it was bound to fall out one day, so as to make room for when his real tusks wanted to come through. Poor Bertie knew nothing of wobbly tusks, or wobbly anything really, and was altogether wobbly himself. It is thanks to Isabella Applebee that he isn't still rolling around on the ground now.

"Are you ok?" asked Izzy.

"My tusk!" Bertie cried. "Gone, gone, *gone!*" he moaned, just as Izzy had done on the first day they had met.

Izzy cried too. She wasn't upset really. But if he was going to cry, then she might as well have a go too.

Once they had finished crying, Izzy picked up the tusk and dragged it into the light for a closer look. It was still very heavy for a baby tooth.

"Don't worry," said Izzy. "It's a baby."

"That makes it an even sadder something to have happened!" Bertie sobbed. "The poor little *baby*."

"Stop that right now," Izzy said, using the tone her parents used when she insisted on bringing Bob to the dining table. "Baby teeth fall out. You had a wobbly tooth."

"Actually," sniffed Bertie, feeling very wobbly himself, "come to think of it, it *had* been wobbling for a while."

Izzy crossed her arms and rolled her eyes as if to say, *I told you so.*

"Have you lost any teeth?" asked Bertie.

"Nope. But I can't wait!"

"Is it a good thing?"

"Yep," she said. "The best thing in the whole world ever."

"Why?"

"Because you are a bigger Bertie and you get to eat wobbly things like jello and custard."

Bertie liked eating just about anything. It didn't matter if it was hard or soft or covered in flaming spikes. However, he had to admit eating wobbly things did sound like fun.

Izzy stood on her tiptoes to give him a congratulatory sort of scratch behind the ears. Then she squealed and pointed.

"Bertie! Look! Tooth!"

Bertie looked in the mirror. There was the smallest fraction of a tusk, peeping out like a bulb in the earth. Yet it was most certainly a brand-new tusk.

"Dodecahedrons!" yelped Bertie, remembering Annabeth with another pang. It was not as sharp this time, but it still hurt. He spun in circles. He flapped his ears and trumpeted. Izzy spun with him and they flapped and trumpeted together. Because they both agreed that it was "the best tooth in the whole world ever."

That night, Bertie and Izzy put the baby tusk out for the Tusk Fairy. It didn't fit beneath Bertie's pillow. So, they put it in a wheelbarrow at the end of the bed. In the morning the wheelbarrow was gone. But in its place was a shiny gold coin. Bertie put the coin in his pocket, and they had soup and jello and custard.

CHAPTER 26

In which Bertie
tells a story

"Can you tell me a story, Bertie?" asked Izzy one night.

Bertie noticed a new spray of freckles dusting her face like cinnamon. She had spent all day outside without her hat. She was tucked up in bed, her hair freshly washed, her yellow ringlets spread out across the pillow in a soggy halo. Bertie took a deep breath and blew hot apple-pie puffs out of his nose until her hair was dry again. It bounced back into shape immediately and her pillow was as warm as if it had just come off a sun-soaked washing line. Bertie licked her ear and nibbled her hair. She smelled sweet and sour in the very best way. Sour like plums and pickles, lemon curd and limes.

Bertie went over to the bookcase and slid one off the shelf. But Izzy shook her head and kicked the covers off.

"Not a story like *that*," she said. "I want a talking one."

Bertie had heard Mr. and Mrs Applebee doing "the talking ones" where they made up a story of their own. But Bertie didn't have any of his own and he didn't know how to make one up, since for that he needed an imagination.

Izzy sighed and sat up. "Just *talk* it, like this: Once upon a time there was a girl and she was the best girl in the whole world ever and she had a rabbit and its name was Rabbit. Or like this…" Izzy took a deep breath. "Once there was a potato it was a ninja potato and it fought bad pineapples and bad tomatoes and more bad pineapples that's all."

"You have a wonderful imagination," sighed Bertie, tucking his tail between his legs. His trunk began to quiver, and he thought he might cry for the disappointment of not having one of his very own. It was the thing he wanted most in the world.

"I like your nose," said Izzy, giggling, forgetting what they were talking about.

Bertie gave a little rumble. He liked her nose, too. He liked everything about Isabella Applebee, except how early she liked to wake up in the morning.

"What's this?" she said, peeling off Bertie's tea cozy and putting it on her head.

"It's a tea cozy."

"Where did you get it?" Izzy mumbled dreamily as she sank down into her pillow.

Bertie thought back to the day when he first put on his tea cozy. It had been the day he had gone to the museum.

"It belonged to someone else, once," said Bertie.

"Who?"

Bertie took a breath, feeling something open up inside him. It was the same feeling that he had gotten when he had taken Izzy for a ride around the garden. As though he were heading into wide open space with no one to guide him, but himself.

"Someone I used to know."

"What happened to him?"

Bertie couldn't say. He closed his eyes. Too afraid to see what was on the other side. "I don't know," he said. "I can't imagine."

Although he didn't dare to try, he was halfway curious. Which is halfway there, as you know. But it didn't much matter. Izzy was all the way asleep and dreaming.

CHAPTER 27

In which Bertie gets the blame

The next morning, Bertie and Izzy were having a tea party. Tea parties were important to Isabella Applebee. Bertie poured out the tea and passed around the sugar bowl.

"One lump or two?" he asked Bob, spooning out some wooden cubes.

Bob didn't seem to like his cup of tea, or the bonnet that Izzy had made him wear for the occasion. He scurried off and hid in the dark space beneath her bed, peering out beneath his long fringe. It was so early that Bertie wished he could crawl beneath and hide in there too, but he wouldn't fit.

"Cookies?" asked Izzy. Bertie finished stirring Rabbit's tea, and handed Izzy the plate of wooden cookies he had arranged. Izzy pushed them away.

"They're not *real* cookies," she said, narrowing her eyes.

Scrambling to her feet, she stood at the door and checked that the coast was clear. Izzy's mother was sitting at the kitchen table, writing a letter. Her father was folding washing. Her goldfish was bubbling around its bowl. She grabbed Bertie by the tail and led him into the hall.

"Cookies," she said, pointing to a tin on a high shelf. She gave Bertie a shove on the bottom. "*Pink* cookies, please."

Bertie squeezed down the hallway and shuffled into the kitchen, trying not to knock things over. He reached up and took the cookie tin off the shelf with his trunk.

Back in her room, he watched as Izzy ripped off the lid. Then Izzy, Bertie, Rabbit and Bob crunched and munched the cookies and sipped tea from their tiny teacups.

Izzy took her own pretend sip and narrowed her eyes at Bertie again. Something was missing.

She grabbed him by the tail and hauled him back out to the hall.

"Milk," she said, pointing to the fridge. "*Cold* milk, please."

Bertie did as he was told and got the milk carton out of the fridge. Izzy's mother looked straight through him, checking the date on the calendar. Izzy's father was ironing his shirts. And Izzy's goldfish was hiding in its china castle.

When all the milk and all the cookies were gone, Izzy stood up.

"Let's go outside," she said, picking up Bob and stomping through the middle of the tea party, treading on plates and spoons. Bertie trotted off behind her as she raced ahead.

Outside, Bertie found Izzy standing on a potato box wearing her father's glasses and best tie. Her father could hardly see without them, which was just as well, since the box was about to collapse and Izzy had used up all the first-aid supplies during her mobile vet clinic.

"We're playing school," she announced when Bertie joined Bob in the sandpit. "Pretend I'm a teacher and you're not a teacher and you go to school but you don't know anything and it's your first day."

Bertie sighed. He still wasn't any good at this game. "Can I have some homework? Where is my lunchbox?"

"Not like *that*." Izzy groaned and dragged Bertie out of the sandpit by his tail. "Like this." She made a sweet-looking face and clasped her hands. "Please, I am new to this school and my name is Rosie Amelia Strawberry and I don't have a home."

Bertie cleared his throat and repeated after her: "Please, I am new to this school and my name is Rosie Amelia...er...Strawberry—that's right—and I don't have a home."

Izzy jumped off the potato box and waved what appeared to be a sword in his face. "Go away, you bad children. You're baddies and we're baddies too!"

"Dodecahedrons!" Bertie yelped.

"Scrub the deck!" she ordered.

"Oh," said Bertie. "Ok." Since now it seemed they were playing pirates. Again.

"No, do it like this: 'Aye aye, Captain!'"

"Aye aye, Captain," said Bertie.

"No, do it like this: 'Aye aye, Captain!'"

"Aye aye, Captain," said Bertie.

"No, do it like this: 'Aye aye, Captain!'"

"Aye aye, Captain!" trumpeted Bertie, raising his trunk in a salute.

"Yarrrr!" Izzy bellowed. "Say 'yarrrrrrrr' like this."

"Yarrrrrrrrrr!" called Bertie.

"No, do it like this: 'yarrrrrrrr!' Say 'yarrrrrrrr' like this."

"Yarrrrrrrrrr!" copied Bertie, just as Izzy had done.

"No, do it like this: 'yarrrrrrrr!' Say 'yarrrrrrrr' like this."

"Yaaaaaaaaaaarrrrrrrrrrrrrrrrrrrrrr!" bellowed Bertie.

The game was interrupted by Izzy's mother. She was holding the empty cookie tin and carton of milk and she was not smiling. Her face was drawn, her jaw was set. She opened her mouth to say something when Izzy extended a grubby finger and pointed to Bertie, "It was *him*."

Bertie gasped. But Izzy's mother just looked straight through him and pointed to the house.

"Time Out," she said. "Now."

That was the problem with being an imaginary
friend: you always got the blame.

As Izzy and Bertie sat in the hallway in the Time
Out Chair, he remembered the first afternoon that
he had spent on The Kitchen Step with Annabeth. It
had been unfair then, and it was unfair now. Bertie
felt the bristles on his neck stand up. He leaned his
head against the wall and listened to the *tick, tick,
tick,* of the clock. Then, "*Cuckoo! Cuckoo! Cuckoo!*"

A stuffed green bird flew out and blared in his
face. Bertie wailed and dropped to his knees, hiding
his eyes beneath his ears. Time and injustice had
snuck up on him once again, and he didn't like them
one bit.

CHAPTER 28

In which Bertie
is a hero

After that, Izzy wasn't allowed any more cookies for a week. Not pink, or plain, or covered in coconut. Not round, square or shaped like a bear. They said it was because they loved her that they had to be so tough sometimes. Bertie thought that being tough was a strange way to show love. From what he had learned, love was something soft and fragile and didn't take kindly to being bossed around.

Yet Izzy had not complained; she had been on her best behavior, since the Royal Show was coming up and she wanted a showbag. Bertie had seen the gold tickets pinned to the fridge.

On the day of the Show, Izzy packed her rabbit in the bag along with their hats and bottles of water.

"It has to stay here," said her father. "You don't want it to get lost in a crowd."

Izzy wailed for her rabbit, her yellow ringlets nodding up and down, but eventually she left it with Bob for safekeeping. Bob did not like that rabbit. He eyed it through his fringe and covered it with straw.

Izzy and Bertie clung to each other as they entered the show gates. He had never seen so many people before. They stared straight through him, their hands full of hot dogs and buttery cobs of corn. Every step he took, he looked out for the flick of a tail or the curve of a spike, although he couldn't see one other Perfect. How strange it is, thought Bertie, to feel alone in a crowd.

To be the only one left. They walked past the showground and a face-painting stall. Past a cart selling hot nuts. Bertie's nose twitched, but Izzy was tugging on his tail and pulling him towards the Farmyard Nursery, in search of the baby animals. On the way, they passed people carving pumpkins, shearing sheep and chopping wood, dogs jumping over hay bales, and children beeping tractor horns.

At the Farmyard Nursery, Izzy held a fuzzy yellow duckling, patted a piglet, and fed a lamb a bottle of milk.

Afterwards, they followed the crowd out of the barn and lined up outside the Grand Pavilion. Bertie ambled wide-eyed through the canopy. There were tables draped with silk ribbons and rosettes piled high with sponge cakes and scones. There were looms and spinning wheels threaded with bright colored yarn. Judges in white coats wandered down the aisles, inspecting flowers and fleeces. There were patchwork quilts and portraits—even faces made from apples and pears. Bertie tried the samples from jars of wild honey and olives and nibbled the plaits of pasta hanging down from the roof. But Izzy seemed bored and stood poking at a scarecrow with a carrot nose and a straw hat.

"Rides, now?" she asked.

Bertie felt his stomach lurch. He had been hoping she hadn't seen them. Outside, they found a big slide, a pirate ship, spinning teacups and bumper cars. They all looked horribly frightening to Bertie, and he would have much rather visited the giant pumpkin display.

Izzy squealed, "Horseys!" and dragged Bertie to the carousel. After two rides on a painted pony called Cascade, she headed to the jumping castle and bounced around like a grasshopper. Bertie watched as she flipped and flopped beside a girl with her face painted like a butterfly. The girl whispered something to her. And when Bertie blinked, the ride was over and Izzy was gone.

It didn't take long for her parents to notice.

"Isabella?" called her mother.

Bertie watched as the kids bounded off the jumping castle, one by one, until it was empty. Izzy did not get off with the others.

"*Isabella*?!" shouted her father.

Bertie hurried around the front of the jumping castle. He loped around to the back.

He looked behind trash cans, under tables and inside a portable toilet. He stood up on his hind legs and tried to get a better view above the crowd. But Izzy was nowhere to be seen. *Flap. Flap. Thump. Flap. Flap. Thump. Flap. Flap. Whump* went his heart.

"*Izzy?*" Bertie called. "Where are you?" He wished that everyone would freeze. That the teacups would stop spinning. That the lights would stop flashing. That the buttons would stop pinging. Things were moving so fast around him. Everything was so loud. But inside, his world was frozen and silent.

Mr. and Mrs Applebee dashed around, shaking people on the sleeve and tapping people on the back, asking anyone if they had seen a girl of three with yellow ringlets anywhere. Soon there were more people searching and calling out for Izzy, and an announcement was made over the loud speaker. But there was still no sign of Isabella Applebee. There was only one thing left to do.

Bertie closed his eyes. His whiskers quivered. He puffed out his cheeks as though he were trying to blow up a balloon. And in a way he was, since it takes curiosity and courage to try and put air inside a balloon. Although what Bertie was really doing was trying to *imagine*. Trying to imagine where Izzy was. What it would be like to be Isabella Applebee. Where he would go if he were in her shoes. This time, there was no one there to do it for him. His Someone was lost. And she needed his help. And just like magic, Bertie closed his eyes and he was *flying*. Although this time, it was for real.

Over the crowd as fast as he could. Ducking and weaving. Clearing bars and around barrels that were only meant for the ponies. *Flap. Flap. Vroom. Flap. Flap. Zoom. Flap. Flap. Ka-boom!*

Bertie went past kids throwing balls into open-mouthed clowns. Past a girl winning a giant panda. Past a boy scooping a rubber duck. Past a man selling custard bombs and unicorn buns. All the way back to the face-painting stand. Because if *he* had been Izzy, bouncing beside that girl on the jumping castle with her face painted, he would have wanted to have his face painted like a butterfly too.

And there was Izzy. Just as he had imagined. Standing forlorn in the showground, surrounded by alpacas, posh poodles and hairless cats all competing for Best In Show. The face-painting stand had closed, so she had wandered to the other side of the dusty track to look at the prize-winning guinea pigs.

"You're not Bob," Bertie heard her say to an

enormous silky specimen with its hair all tied in bows. It had a "Grandest Guinea" ribbon draped around its cushion. Izzy slumped on a hay bale and began to weep. Bertie squeezed through the crowd and scooped her up with his trunk, hoisting her high above the sea of heads.

"B-b-b-b-b-bertie?"

Her forehead was damp with sweat. Wet curls plastered to her face.

"Hello," said Bertie.

"I...just...wanted...to be...a...*butterfly!*" Izzy gasped through ragged sobs.

"I know," soothed Bertie.

"I...want...to...go...*home!*"

"You're almost there," said Bertie, seeing her parents up ahead. He knew that her parents were her real home. When they got closer, he put her on the ground and nudged her in the right direction.

"Daddy!" she cried. "Mommy!"

Mr. and Mrs Applebee dropped to their knees. Their faces were pale and their eyes rubbed red. Bertie could tell that despite their never having said a word to him, and even though they looked straight through him, he had something in common with Mr. and Mrs Applebee. Izzy was their Someone, too. Isabella Applebee was important to Mr. and Mrs Applebee. The most important thing in the world. The Applebees loved Izzy, despite their strange ways of showing it sometimes. Bertie thought there was nothing quite so strange or important as love. That it wasn't always soft and fragile as he had thought. But that it was tough and fierce. Unbreakable.

CHAPTER 29

In which Bertie finds a Ferris wheel

Bertie watched as the Applebees went into the Great Hall to choose a showbag. Weeks ago, Izzy had already told him the one that she wanted: The White Rabbit Bag. It was full of magic tricks, stickers, pencils, coloring-in books, bouncy balls and of course—*rabbits*. There were rabbit ears, rabbit tails, toy rabbits and even a rabbit money box. She had chosen it weeks ago, but last night she had been having second thoughts and was tossing up between The White Rabbit Bag and Ben's Big Cookie Bag.

Finally, she had told her parents she needed *two* showbags, because her friend Bertie needed one too.

"Who is Bertie?" her mother had asked.

"He's my best friend in the whole world!"

"Does he go to Nursery School?"

"Yes! And he carries my bag!"

"Well, Bertie sounds like a very nice fellow."

Izzy had sprung upon this opportunity to say that Bertie was especially large, and so they might actually need to get *three* bags: The White Rabbit Bag and two of the bags with cookies in them as otherwise he would get hungry, and he always cried when he was hungry. But her parents had said that they were not sure that Bertie's parents would be happy about that, and that if Izzy wanted, she could share *her* bag with Bertie. Izzy had crossed her arms and whined.

"But Bertie doesn't even *like* rabbits."

"Well then, Bertie will just have to get his own showbag another time, won't he?"

Bertie had been rather upset by this, since he *did* like rabbits. Izzy quite obviously just didn't want to share. And he was sure that if Mr. and Mrs Applebee knew Bertie had been standing right behind them listening they wouldn't have been so quick to dismiss the idea.

Now, as Bertie was wandering around the showground on his own, it wasn't the showbags that caught his attention. It was the Ferris wheel. The giant ring, lit with lanterns and stripy carriages spinning gently. He watched the boys and girls sitting in the very top carriage waving to their friends below. Bertie stumped his way to try and get a closer look. When he reached the ticket booth, something *else* caught his attention. Bertie ran in a circle, flapping his ears.

Is it? It couldn't be. But it is! Or is it? Could it really be? It is!

And it was! Mr. Confetti's ice-cream truck parked right beneath the Ferris wheel.

More astonishing still was that Mr. Confetti saw Bertie. He didn't look straight through him like everybody else except Izzy, but right at him. He smiled and beckoned to Bertie, so Bertie took his place in the line.

As he waited for his turn, he suddenly felt nervous. He didn't know what to do. He had never ordered an ice-cream before. In fact, he had never bought anything before. But then he remembered Charles Dimple saying that Mr. Confetti picked

your favorite flavor for you, without you having to ask.

As soon as Bertie made his way to the front counter, Mr. Confetti began scooping out smooth spheres of ice-cream and piling them into an enormous waffle cone. It wasn't a berry-swirl waffle cone that Mr. Confetti had chosen, as he always did for Charles. It was *green*. With something sprinkled on top. A wonderful something. A *magical* something. A salty, crunchy something.

Bertie fished around in his pocket until he found the shiny gold coin that the Tusk Fairy had left for him. Shaking it off, Bertie put it on the counter. Mr. Confetti picked it up and rubbed it on his candy-striped coat.

"Heads or tails?"

"Tails," said Bertie, thumping his own.

Mr. Confetti flicked the coin into the air, caught it, then cupped it on the back of one hand.

"Tails it is!" he said, revealing the coin then sending it spinning back across the counter.

Bertie trumpeted and put the coin back in his pocket. Mr. Confetti took off his straw hat, bowed and handed Bertie his ice-cream. His Perfect Pistachio ice-cream.

Bertie's tongue quivered as he took his first lick. The bristles on his neck stood up, and his new tusk tingled. Bertie took another lick. Then another. Rolling his tongue around and around his ice-cream until it was all gone and all his bristles lay flat again. Then he crunched down the cone. "*Grum, grum, grum.*" He rumbled so much that the pavement shook, and a lady's hat went crooked. And that was how he made another magical discovery: that pistachios were important to Bertie.

When it was all gone, with only some green crunchy bits sticking to his whiskers, Bertie looked around him. The bristles on the back of his neck stood up again, since he was sure he could see Charles Dimple riding on the top of the Ferris wheel. Memories soared through him, lifting up his heart like a pair of bright white wings in a dull gray sky. Although this boy looked much older, he was still the same in all the important ways. He was wearing something on his head. Some sort of hat... no, a tea cozy! It was definitely Charles.

Bertie thought of calling out. Yet he wasn't sure Charles would be able to hear him, since he couldn't see him anymore.

But of one thing Bertie was sure: Charles Dimple was happy.

And Bertie was, too.

It truly was a magical night.

CHAPTER 30

In which Bertie is almost-nearly Everywhere

One day, Bertie looked up and was surprised to find that Isabella had grown older, too.

Izzy still had yellow ringlets and lived in the yellow house, although there were new people living next door. Annabeth Arch had long since moved away to design The Greatest Library In The World. Izzy was still just as sweet and sour as always but some things had changed. She never played in the sandpit, and she didn't want to be called Izzy anymore: that was too babyish. These days, she only answered to the name "Bella." She didn't steal many cookies—she bought them herself with the money she got for losing her baby teeth. But she was often stealing Bertie's spectacles, since she thought they made her look sophisticated. Which they did. Plus, she hardly ever got jam on her face these days. It tended to land lower down, on her school collar.

The other biggest change was that Bertie spent most days on his own.

Like today, when Bella was busy making plans of her own.

"I'm going away for a bit," Bella said as she munched on her toast.

Bertie stopped nibbling the crumbs on the floor and sat up. "Where are you going?"

"To the city with some friends," she said.

Bertie chewed on his lip.

"Not for ever-never?" he asked.

"No Bertie," said Bella, rubbing him between the ears. "Not forever and ever. I'll be back soon, and I'll bring you back a present."

Bertie flew around the kitchen: *Flap. Flap. Whee! Flap. Flap. Eee! Flap. Flap. Squee!*

Bertie liked presents. Last time, she had brought him a bag of pistachios, two pine cones and a kazoo.

"Don't forget to feed Bob II and fill up his water bowl."

Bertie sighed. He and Bob II had never seen whisker to whisker. He was even snootier than Bob I had been. "Will you send me a postcard?"

"I will," said Bella, giving him a scratch and slinging her bag over her shoulder.

"Wait," said Bertie. "There's something you've forgotten." He reached out and gave her his umbrella. "In case it rains."

"Thank you," she said, kissing him on the trunk.

He blew hot apple-pie puffs into her cheek. "And thank *you*," he said.

That night, Bertie couldn't sleep. There was something in the air. The wind was restless and the night crackled with possibility. Or was that Bob II eating nuts in his hutch outside?

Either way, Bertie's mind gamboled ahead of him, despite his heavy legs. He was tired, having traveled so far. Although a part of him was just waking up. He put on his spectacles, then fished around in his pockets for some of the other gifts that Annabeth had given him. He pulled out a pencil and his notebook. The pages were crisp and blank. The curtains rose and fell like waves around him. The air smelled of sweet new jasmine for it was summer again.

And for the second time that day, Bertie looked up.

Then he closed his eyes and *imagined*.

She began as a spark. An idea. To start with, she was no more than a speck of gold dust floating on the wind, bobbing across an ocean, tumbling down a waterfall, hurtling towards her destiny like a shooting star. When she finally arrived, damp and a little weary, it was late and Bertie was in bed staring blankly at the sky.

There is something missing, he was thinking. But what is it?

The spark flickered on the windowsill, watching the large huddle of fur searching for an idea, unaware that one was right beside him. Creeping closer, the spark glimmered on Bertie's shoulder, trying to see what he was making. It was a list.

This particular list was labeled: THE PERFECT FRIEND. Although it was more like a job description than a list. At the top of Bertie's list were PICNICS. Picnics were important to Bertie. Beneath picnics was another word: SMALL. His perfect friend would be SMALL. And by SMALL, Bertie meant that his friend should be small enough to hide beneath him in a storm. But not so small that they would get lost in his breakfast. BREAKFAST being third on the list. Not to be eaten for breakfast, of course, but to share it with, on those days when Bella was feeling especially sophisticated and independent, and would rather eat alone. Independence was important to Isabella Applebee, now that she was old enough to ride on a Ferris wheel by herself. And something for eating pistachios with—a beak or perhaps a bill. Maybe some talons to crack them open and for climbing trees while playing hide and seek. Hide-and-seeking being one of Bertie's hobbies after all. Furthermore, his perfect friend would have strings like an instrument. That thrummed when they flapped and strummed when they snored. A bit like a harp—but better. Patience, kindness and a sense of humor were also essential.

They should enjoy discussing important matters such as cosmic theories, constellations, mongooses and other members of the Herpestidae family, architecture, cookies, and the very best showbags. An interest in gymnastics was not preferable, yet not actively discouraged. (In other words, he would not hold it against them. And in fact, he was getting quite good at doing somersaults if you tilted your head and squinted.)

It's me, crackled the spark. *Or it could be.*

Glowing with excitement, the spark fizzed and hummed around Bertie's head. *Pick me, pick me!* Until the beast trapped it with his mind like a firefly in a jar. Once inside, something powerful began to take shape. The idea stretched and swelled until *poof!*

An image flashed before Bertie. He saw someone. Or something. In his room. A sort of *bird*. It was a little wobbly and smudged around the edges. But here it was.

His mouth fell open as he stepped back to admire his work. He had never seen anything so grand. So *perfect*. Bertie and the bird stood looking at each other, their hearts beating together like the two wings of a butterfly.

"Where did you come from?"

"Nowhere," she chirped.

Bertie's tail thumped. His heart leaped. Because he had Somewhere just for her, right on top of his head. It was a Perfect place. Just the place in which to go Everywhere.

But first, she needed a name.

"*Ah-tish-oo!*" sneezed the bird.

So now that you know about Tish, he is yours. Tish, who is quick like a mongoose, but lazy like a bear. Tish, who is heavy like a mammoth, but has a heart like a feather. Tish, whose small, stumpy wings can almost-nearly fly. Tish, who cries when he is happy or hungry or mad.

Say hello to him for me when you see him. For he was once mine.

He may look different now. He may go by a different name. But he is still the same in all the important ways. And you *will* meet him, if you look hard enough. It is only a matter of time. Or you might meet Someone Else, because thanks to his great imagination, Tish is no longer the last of his kind.

Acknowledgements:

Thank you to my publisher, Nancy Conescu, for inspiring this book and encouraging me to write it. You truly are the Perfect friend. Thank you, Alex Wyatt, for being my Someone and gifting me a life beyond my wildest imaginings. Thank you, Kiah Thomas, for making me laugh and for making me a better writer. And thank you, Alyson and Jim, my parents, for everything.

Published in 2021 by Berbay Publishing Pty Ltd
First US edition published in 2022

PO Box 133
Kew East
Victoria 3102 Australia

Text © Edwina Wyatt
Illustrations @ Odette Barberousse

Publisher: Nancy Conescu
Designer: Akiko Chan
Printed by Everbest Printing in China

Cataloguing-in-publication data is available from the National Library of Australia

catalogue.nla.gov.au

ISBN 978-1-922610-52-2

Visit our catalogue at www.berbaybooks.com